VOYAGE *of the* SPARROWHAWK

VOYAGE of the SPARROWHAWK

NATASHA FARRANT

NORTON YOUNG READERS
An Imprint of W. W. Norton & Company
Independent Publishers Since 1923

Text copyright © 2020 by Natasha Farrant
First American Edition 2021

Map by David Dean

All rights reserved
Printed in the United States of America

For information about permission to reproduce selections from this book,
write to Permissions, W. W. Norton & Company, Inc.,
500 Fifth Avenue, New York, NY 10110

For information about special discounts for bulk purchases,
please contact W. W. Norton Special Sales at
specialsales@wwnorton.com or 800-233-4830

Manufacturing by Lakeside Book Manufacturing
Book design by Beth Steidle
Production manager: Beth Steidle

ISBN 978-1-324-01972-5

W. W. Norton & Company, Inc., 500 Fifth Avenue, New York, N.Y. 10110
www.wwnorton.com

W. W. Norton & Company Ltd., 15 Carlisle Street, London W1D 3BS

2 4 6 8 9 0 7 5 3 1

For Jane, Eleanor, Matilda and Julia.

In memory of Dobby, a most excellent Chihuahua.

"I ought to say," explained Pooh as they walked down to the shore of the island, "that it isn't just an ordinary sort of boat. Sometimes it's a Boat, and sometimes it's more of an Accident. It all depends."

"Depends on what?"

"On whether I'm on the top of it or underneath it."

—A. A. MILNE

As wonderful as dogs can be, they are famous for missing the point.

—JEAN FERRIS

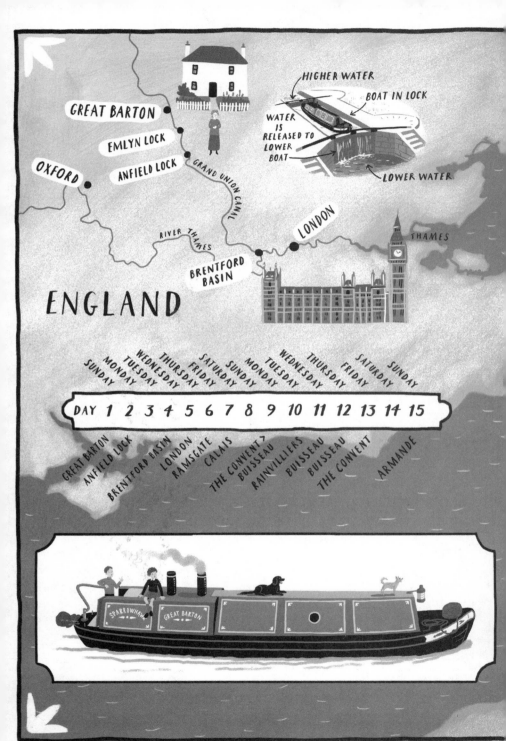

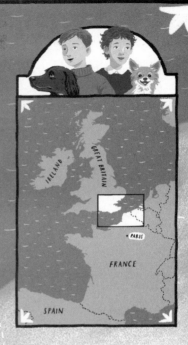

A MAP OF THE VOYAGE of the SPARROWHAWK

RAMSGATE

DUNKIRK

CALAIS

STRAIT OF DOVER

HÔTEL

CANAL D'AIRE

FRANCE

LILLE

RIVER ESCAUT

ST. MATTHIEU

RAINVILLIERS

RIVER SCARPE

BUISSEAU

CANAL DU NORD

BAIE DE LA SOMME

RIVER SOMME

ARMANDE

PROLOGUE

Ben

Once, a long time ago, there was a boy called Ben. He lived in a big, gray orphanage on the edge of a big, gray town, where the orphans ate gray food and wore gray clothes and went barefoot even in winter—which was miserable but also quite lucky, because if Ben had worn shoes, most of the things in this book would probably never have happened.

Every Sunday, the orphans were made to go for a long walk along the canal that ran through the town. And one Sunday, when he was four years old, Ben cut his foot on a piece of glass and it hurt so much that he stopped right in the middle of the towpath and began to cry. Now you might have thought the other orphans would stop for him, but the orphanage had strict rules about being late, and the orphans were scared of getting into trouble. They just carried on walking until Ben was quite alone except for one other orphan.

Sam was eleven years old, tough as the boots he didn't have, and really couldn't care less about trouble. In fact, the people who ran the orphanage said that, most of the time, Sam *was* the trouble.

"Stop crying and show me your foot," he ordered. Ben, whose awe of Sam was absolute, did as he was told.

"I'm going to pull the glass out," said Sam. "Are you brave?"

"Yes," said Ben, then howled at the pain.

Sam grinned, threw away the glass and crouched down so Ben could climb on his back.

"Jump on!"

They came to a bend in the canal. A new narrowboat had arrived, and a man sat in her hold, painting a lion on a wooden pub sign. Sam stopped to watch. Ben slid off his back and hopped to the edge of the water.

The boat was red and green, with her name, *Sparrowhawk*, painted in gold on a scarlet panel. Above the letters, a bird of prey flew, tough and graceful, orange eyes glinting and blue-gray wings outstretched. Ben reached out to touch it.

"Careful you don't fall in," said the man. "What happened to your foot?"

The man's name was Nathan Langton. He walked with a stick, and he had a beard and a soft felt hat and an old dog called Bessie who farted a lot. He cleaned Ben's foot and bandaged it, then gave the boys tea and let Ben play with his paints while Sam explored the boat.

After the boys had gone, Nathan sat for a long time on the edge of the canal, thinking.

The following day, he visited the orphanage to bring the boys a paint box. He saw that Sam's face was bruised from the beating he'd received for being late, and that the bandage on Ben's foot had come off.

He went back to his boat and thought some more.

Ever since his leg was crushed between the *Sparrowhawk* and a boatyard quay, Nathan had earned his living by painting. Shop signs, pub signs, planters, pots ... whatever people wanted painted, Nathan painted it. In fine weather, he worked outside in the hold. When it rained, he worked in the cabin.

"Could do with a change, anyway," he muttered to himself.

He covered the hold with a sloping roof into which he cut two windows. He put in a door on to a small foredeck and laid a floor. He built a wooden bench with drawers beneath it for his clothes, a bookcase for his collection of Dickens novels, shelves for his pots and brushes. He put in a stove and set up an easel.

It was the first beautiful room Nathan had ever had, and he loved it.

After he had built the workshop, Nathan went to work on the cabin. When he had finished, he went shopping. And then he returned to the orphanage for the boys.

A month after Ben and Sam first visited the *Sparrowhawk*, they came back and called it home. In the cabin they found boots, soft with wear and almost the right size, socks to go with them, warm sweaters, trousers and jackets. Best of all, built into the wall one above the other, they each had their very own berth, Sam on top and Ben below. Nathan had painted their names on wooden panels hung above the pillows, with a bird for each of the boys—a quick bright kingfisher for Sam, a robin with a bandaged foot for Ben.

"We can change it if you like, now your foot's better," Nathan said.

But Ben adored the robin, just as he adored the *Sparrowhawk*.

Sam was freckled and sandy-haired and full of mischief. Ben was dark-haired, with big, gray eyes and a slow, shy smile. The two boys couldn't have been more different, but they loved each other like brothers and they loved Nathan as a father. As the *Sparrowhawk* drove out of town in the morning sun, Ben hugged Bessie close and felt his heart swell fit to burst.

PROLOGUE

Lotti

About four years after Nathan adopted Sam and Ben, farther south near the small town of Great Barton, a man and a woman in a smart sports car paused at the gates of their country estate.

"We should stay," said the woman.

"My love," her husband replied. "Look at the sky!"

Their names were Théophile and Isobel St. Rémy, and they were on their way to an airfield, to go up in an airplane. Théophile was French, with a head of wild curls and twinkly brown eyes. Isobel was English and fair, with creamy skin, which smelled of roses. They were like people in a fairy tale, these two, kind and loving as well as beautiful and rich, and blessed with an adored eight-year-old daughter called Lotti, who had the wild hair and impetuous nature of her papa, and the blue eyes and kindness of her mama. It was the thought of Lotti that made Isobel hesitate now. Lotti would have loved to go up in an airplane, but she was stuck in bed with a streaming cold, being looked after by the servants and an old cat called Queen Victoria.

"She was so disappointed," said Isobel in the car. "Let's all go together when she's better."

Théophile hesitated. He also hated to leave Lotti. But then he looked again at the blue, blue sky.

"It's just such a perfect day for flying . . ."

So they went. And a terrible thing happened, but . . . well, it's like with Ben's shoes. If they had stayed, there would be no story.

The storm came from nowhere, people said, which was stupid. Storms are created when a center of low pressure develops with a system of high pressure surrounding it. They do not come from *nowhere*.

But still. Wherever it came from, the storm did in the airplane, and it did in Lotti's parents.

In their will, Théophile and Isobel left everything they owned to their daughter, and appointed Isobel's much older brother, Hubert, to look after both Lotti and her fortune until she was twenty-one.

Poor Lotti ...

On the outside, Hubert Netherbury and his wife, Vera, seemed dull but dependable, which was why the St. Rémys had chosen them as guardians years before, when Lotti was a little baby. But underneath their bland exterior they were snobs who hated scandal but loved money. As a young man, Hubert had been ambitious, but the success in business that had made Théophile very rich had eluded him. He and Vera lived in a small house, with only one servant, who doubled as a cook, and over the years even their blandness had faded. By the time Isobel and Théophile died, Vera's face had become mean and pinched, and Hubert's had the sly and sullen expression of a bully. They had disliked Isobel and Théophile, and disapproved of their lifestyle, but they were delighted to come and live in their house. Barton Lacey, with its eight bedrooms and string of reception rooms, its famous gardens and extensive woodlands, was *exactly* the sort of home they felt they had always deserved.

The only problem was Lotti, who just by existing reminded them that Barton Lacey was not really theirs.

They might have tolerated a quiet child, but for weeks after the funeral, Lotti did nothing but cry. She had nightmares and screamed for her parents. She refused to eat. She locked herself in her room with Queen Victoria and would not come out. She informed her uncle and aunt that she hated them.

She gave them her cold.

Perhaps, if life had not disappointed them, Hubert and Vera might have been kind, but it had, and they were not. They did not hold Lotti while she wept or tell her that they loved her. They did not ask Cook to prepare her favorite meals. When Lotti finally came out of her room, puffy with tears, they made her take her meals alone in the kitchen, and they banned Queen Victoria from the house. When this made Lotti cry all over again, they told her she was wicked. And when summer ended they sent her far away to a gloomy boarding school, just after the war had started.

In all of this, only one person had comforted Lotti: her French grandmother, Camille St. Rémy, or Moune as Lotti called her. She came for the funeral, and for a few days Lotti clung to her. When she left, Moune promised that she would write every week, and that every summer Lotti would spend the month of August with her in France in her timber-framed house overlooking the river at Armande, as she had with her parents every summer since she was born.

But Moune's letters stopped when Lotti went to school. The war went on, and there were no holidays in France. There were, in fact, no holidays at all for Lotti.

Her life, which had been so rich and full of love, was reduced almost exclusively to the grounds of her school, where she remained for the next four and a half years, homesick, lonely and absolutely friendless.

Then, in the spring of 1919, she got herself expelled.

Which is where our story begins.

PART I

Chapter One

It was the first April since the war. The sky was blue, the sun was shining, the scent of blossoms wafted on the breeze. Birds sang, and the people of Great Barton smiled at each other in the street.

A cheerful day, then, with the world waking up to the possibility that all was not cold and dark and fighting. As Ben ran across the meadows toward the canal with his dog, Elsie, at his heels and a rucksack on his back, he felt almost happy.

It was just over eight months since Nathan had gone to France, to visit Sam in the army hospital where he was being treated for a head wound. Eight months almost to the day since the letter came from the farmer with whom Nathan had been staying, to say that the hospital had been bombed and that Nathan had been killed.

Just under eight months since the telegram came from the War Office saying Sam was missing. The longest, hardest eight months of Ben's life, but today things were changing.

Today, Ben was back in charge.

When Nathan went to France, rather than leave Ben and Elsie alone on the *Sparrowhawk* as Ben had wanted, he had trusted them to the care of a local woman, Mercy Jenkins. Mercy had been kind. After Nathan died, rather than put Ben in the care of the local authorities, who would have taken Elsie away and sent Ben back to an orphanage, she let him stay on with her.

"Just until we hear what's happened to his brother," she wrote to her husband away at the front. But then Mercy's husband had also been killed, and a few months later she decided to leave Great Barton to go and live with her sister on a farm in Wales.

"You can come with me, if you like," she had said to Ben. "We'll need a hard-working lad."

But Ben had no intention of going with Mercy. What Ben wanted was to live on the *Sparrowhawk* and wait for Sam to come home.

"Thanks, but I think I'll stay."

"You can't stay on your boat alone, Ben, you're too young."

"I won't be alone!" Ben smiled, as widely as he could. "I was about to tell you! I got a letter from the War Office."

Mercy frowned. "I didn't see no letter."

"Well, I got one," said Ben. "And it said that Sam's coming home!"

Mercy still looked unconvinced, but he could see that she wanted to believe him.

"When?" she asked.

"Soon. A few days maybe." Ben's smile was so wide now it hurt.

"All right," said Mercy. "I'll speak to Albert. Ask him to keep an eye out for you until Sam gets back."

Albert was Albert Skinner, a local police constable and an acquaintance of Mercy's. And while Ben would rather not have anyone keep an eye out for him, least of all a policeman, he could see it was the only way Mercy would allow him to stay on the *Sparrowhawk* alone.

"Thanks," he had said. "I'll be sure to tell him if I need anything."

And with that Mercy had been satisfied. She had left Great Barton that morning on the train, and now Ben was on his way to the *Sparrowhawk*.

Ben reached the edge of the meadow, ducked through a gap in the hedge onto the towpath, ran past the allotments and the bench near the railway bridge where ex-soldiers liked to drink and play cards, round a bend in the canal past a lonely cottage—and there she was, the *Sparrowhawk*. Not as bright as when Nathan had left, in need of a scrub and a lick of paint, but to Ben as welcoming as the most solid of houses.

He whistled for Elsie, who bounced toward him then stopped in her tracks, baring her teeth.

"What's got into you, you daft dog? We're home!"

Elsie growled, black fur hackling.

"Suit yourself." Ben shrugged. "I'm going on board."

He jumped onto the aft deck, put down his rucksack, pulled the key to the cabin hatch from its front pouch— and paused.

If the hatch stayed closed, he could pretend that behind it everything was as it should be. Nathan painting in the workshop, Sam reading on his berth. "Here's trouble," Nathan would say as Ben jumped down into the cabin, and then he would push a pile of neglected schoolbooks across the fold-down table. "Lessons aren't going to learn themselves, lad."

Ben leaned his head against the hatch and blinked hard. With a quiet thud and a click of claws, Elsie landed beside him on the deck. Ben gave himself a shake.

"You're right," he said, and put the key in the lock. "Let's go in."

He knew as soon as he pushed back the hatch that something was wrong. There was too much light in the cabin. It was only ever that bright if the door to Nathan's workshop was open—and since Nathan had been gone, though Ben had visited the *Sparrowhawk* many times, he had only set foot in the workshop once, when the pain of missing Nathan had been so overwhelming that he had closed the door and never opened it again.

Ben's mind raced.

Who had opened the door? And how had they got in?

The cabin hatch was locked by a padlock from the outside, so they must have gone in from the foredeck. But only one person other than Ben had the key to that, which meant that . . .

Sam was home!

Ben hurled himself through the hatch, tripped over Elsie on the top step, tumbled down the rest and landed in a painful heap on the cabin floor.

A voice spoke, but it was a girl's voice, not his brother's.

"Please," the girl said. "Hide me. It's a matter of life or death."

The girl, of course, was Lotti, though Ben didn't know this yet.

She stood before him in the cabin, flushed from running, the skirt of her old-fashioned sailor suit dirty and torn, her long hair unraveling from its braids. Slung across her body, she carried a canvas satchel.

The satchel was wriggling.

Ben, doubly winded by his fall and the disappointment that Lotti was not Sam, could only stare. Elsie growled, her golden eyes fixed on the satchel.

The satchel jumped.

"It's no good," announced Lotti. "I'm going to have to let him out. You'd better hold on to your dog."

Quite composed, she sat down on Ben's bunk, pulled the satchel's shoulder strap over her head and laid the bag down beside her. Ben finally recovered the power of speech.

"Let who out? What are you talking about?" His voice was high with indignation. Who was this girl, and how dare she intrude like this on his boat? "I don't even know what you're doing here!"

"Shh," Lotti begged. "You *must* be quiet."

Ben *wanted* to say that this was his boat and he would make as much noise as he liked, but now curiosity was getting the better of indignation. Lotti was undoing the satchel's buckles, making tender cooing sounds as she did so. Elsie quivered and stepped closer. Ben slipped his fingers through her collar and craned forward to look.

"It's all right," Lotti whispered into the bag. "No one's going to hurt you."

Ben and Elsie watched in astonishment as a small, black nose emerged from the satchel, then a slim, toffee-colored snout. The nose twitched. A thin paw appeared, then another, followed by surprisingly robust shoulders and the rest of the head, with eyes like black marbles and ears like enormous bat wings, which would have made Ben laugh if the creature hadn't been so very pitiful.

"It's a dog," he said unnecessarily, before adding, "He's very thin."

"That," said Lotti darkly, "is because he's been very badly treated."

Elsie began to whine, soft little cries Ben recognized as words of comfort, and he relaxed his hold on her. Still whining, Elsie advanced on the little dog, who shrank back, flattening his enormous ears. Elsie pressed closer, sniffed him all over, then rather bossily began to lick him clean.

"They've made friends!" Lotti beamed, then turned to Ben. "Isn't that wonderful? I'm Lotti, by the way. I live up at Barton Lacey."

"I'm Ben," said Ben. "I live here. And you still haven't told me what you're doing on my boat."

Lotti, he noted, didn't look the least bit repentant.

"Do you know a man called Malachy Campbell?" she asked. "Short and red, with a nose like a potato?"

"Everyone knows Malachy Campbell," said Ben impatiently. "He's Great Barton's most famous crook. Look, I don't know where this is going, but . . ."

"Would you mind just stepping up on deck and looking to see if he's out there? If he's not, I promise we'll be on our way. I have to get home soon anyway. It's very important that I'm not late, especially today. But Malachy Campbell is chasing me."

This was not how Ben had imagined his homecoming. He had been looking forward to reclaiming the *Sparrowhawk*, unpacking, making her cozy again for him and Elsie.

This was . . . annoying.

But also interesting.

He leaned forward. "Why is Malachy Campbell chasing you?"

Lotti grinned. "Because I stole his dog."

Chapter Two

"*You stole Malachy Campbell's dog?*"

"Oh, please don't shout! You'll upset him."

Ben lowered his voice. "You stole Malachy Campbell's dog?"

"Very successfully." Lotti bounced happily on the berth and brought her legs up to sit cross-legged, looking perfectly at home. "I can tell you all about it, if you like, but I warn you, in the eyes of the police, that would make you an accomplice." She paused to think. "You may actually be an accomplice already. Technically, you may be harboring a fugitive. And hiding stolen goods. The dog being the goods. And also, I suppose, a fugitive. But I promise, if the police come, I'll tell them it's all my fault. And to be frank, I don't think Mr. Campbell is the sort of person who *would* call the police. Shall I continue?"

Ben hesitated. On the one hand, he really didn't want Malachy Campbell or the police or anyone to come round the *Sparrowhawk* asking questions. On the other . . .

"*Why* did you steal his dog?"

"Well, it's a long story," said Lotti. "Could he have some water first? And food? And please can you check Mr. Campbell isn't out there? It would put my mind at rest."

Ben climbed back up to the aft deck and looked up and down the towpath.

"Empty," he confirmed.

Back in the cabin, he took two bowls from a cupboard in the galley, filled one with dog biscuits and the other with water, and put them both on the floor. Elsie fell to eating immediately. Lotti placed the little dog on the ground beside her, and Elsie shuffled aside to make room for him.

"Isn't that sweet?" sighed Lotti. "Your dog is lovely. What sort is she?"

"Mostly spaniel, I think. We rescued her as a puppy, so we've never really known."

"This one is a Chihuahua. I've decided to call him Federico."

"The theft . . . ?" Ben said.

Lotti wrapped her arms round her knees.

"I suppose," she mused, "it all started when I stabbed the sewing mistress."

Ben's head started to swim. "Stabbed . . . ?"

"Only with a needle," Lotti explained hurriedly. "To get expelled. I wanted to come home so badly, you see. I'd been away at school for so long, longer even than the war, since my aunt and uncle sent me there after my parents died in an airplane crash when I was eight. And I was sort of used to it—I mean, it was miserable but *bearable*, in a prisony sort of way—but then this new girl came, Veronica Smedley, and locked me in the coal cellar."

Ben was confused. "Why?"

"I laughed at her," admitted Lotti. "She slipped in the mud playing lacrosse. It wasn't nice of me, I know, but she *did* look funny covered in mud. Anyway, it made her furious. So first she told all the girls they shouldn't speak to me, and then she got them to play pranks on me, and one of the pranks was locking me in the coal cellar. Ben, you look lost. Don't you go to school?"

Ben thought about this. Because they moved around so much, Nathan had always taught his boys at home on the *Sparrowhawk*. When Ben went to live with Mercy, she had vaguely made him attend the Great Barton school but Ben, used to a lifetime of freedom, hadn't loved it. Now that he was living alone, he thought he might go back to learning alone.

"No," he said. "I don't."

"Then you don't understand how properly horrible bullies can be. Veronica made them keep me all night in the coal cellar, and it was one of the loneliest nights of my life, almost as bad as when my parents died. Have you ever been lonely, Ben?"

"I lived in an orphanage until I was four," Ben replied quietly. "And for the last eight months, I've been living alone with a stranger."

Lotti nodded. "Then you do understand. I couldn't *breathe* for loneliness at school, and the worst thing was none of the teachers cared. There was no point telling my aunt and uncle, because they wouldn't have cared either, but I couldn't go on like that. And Papa always said, if you don't like something, you should try to change it. So first I tried to run away."

"Where to?" asked Ben. "Back to Barton?"

Lotti hesitated, but it was too painful to explain that she had wanted to run all the way to France, to Moune, who didn't write but was the only person left who had loved her once.

"Yes," she said. "Back to Barton. I made it to the station, but the last train had gone, and they caught me. So then I realized the only way I would leave is if I got expelled. Hence stabbing the sewing mistress." She paused, remembering the feel of her needle piercing the sewing mistress's arm. There had been screams, and blood. "It was very satisfying."

Ben was speechless, equal parts admiring and appalled.

"What did your aunt and uncle say?"

But this was something else Lotti didn't want to talk about—Hubert Netherbury's rage at Lotti's scandalous behavior, the hard, humiliating slap across the face she had received at Great Barton station when she returned from school, in full view of the other passengers.

"They were a bit cross," she said airily. "But the plan worked, because Uncle Hubert says now I'm nearly thirteen and don't have to go to school by law, there's no point wasting money on my education and I should be learning to Make Myself Useful to My Aunt instead." Lotti rolled her eyes. "I have to do things like tidy her writing desk and sewing box, and mend clothes for the jumble sale at the Women's Institute fête. She is *obsessed* with the Women's Institute fête. She is running it this year and Lady Clarion, whom she worships because she is a proper aristocrat, is on the committee. The fête is to raise funds for returned servicemen and Lady Clarion says it is our patriotic duty to make as much money as possible, and Aunt Vera is desperate for her approval. Aunt Vera has this thing about Barton Lacey not really being hers—it's actually mine—and she sees the fête as her way into high society. It's not till June, but she already keeps having all these committee ladies in for awful coffee mornings where I have to hand round sandwiches. To be honest, I do wonder sometimes if it was worth being expelled from school for this, but then—Ben, you're looking impatient."

"I'm just wondering what this has to do with the dog," Ben said honestly.

"I'm getting to that! The point is, Aunt Vera can only put up with me for a few hours at a time. So in the afternoons, as long as I don't behave *scandalously*, I'm free as a bird to wander around and explore, and *while* I was exploring I noticed that Malachy Campbell kept poor little Federico in a tiny dirty cage in his yard. And then I followed him for a bit, because he was taking Federico all around town trying to sell him, but nobody wanted him. I mean"—Lotti dropped her voice—"even I can see he's quite *odd*-looking, especially when he's so thin. So I said to myself, if Mr. Campbell hasn't sold that poor dog in five days, I will rescue him. And he didn't. So *I* did."

"But *how?*" Ben was enthralled.

"Well, that bit was quite easy," said Lotti. "All I had to do was steal a crowbar from Zachy—Zachy is our gardener, and a darling—and then wait for Mr. Campbell to go out, climb over the wall of his yard, force open the cage, pick up Federico and *run!*"

"But why are you *here*, on the *Sparrowhawk?*"

"Because Mr. Campbell came back and saw what I'd done, so he ran after me. Luckily, even carrying Federico, I'm much faster than him. He never got close! But then I got tired, and I saw your boat and I just . . . jumped on."

"How did you get in?"

Lotti shifted guiltily and glanced toward Nathan's workshop. Ben followed her gaze and winced. A trail of muddy footprints led right across the floor to the door, which was hanging ajar. The gardener's crowbar lay on the floor beside it.

Ben stood up and closed the door between the cabin and the workshop.

"Are you cross?" whispered Lotti.

Ben thought about this carefully. Nathan's workshop! He had avoided it for months, and she had just breezed in, traipsed through it as if it were nothing. He *should* be cross. He was definitely upset. And yet at the same time, he knew that Nathan and Sam would both have loved the story of the rescued Chihuahua . . .

"No," he admitted.

Lotti breathed a sigh of relief, then burst out laughing. "Ben, what *is* your dog doing?"

Elsie had climbed on to Ben's berth and was turning round in tight circles on the mattress. As they watched, she curled into a ball and pulled the blanket over her head with her teeth.

Ben smiled and reached into the blanket to scratch her ears. "It means it's going to rain."

"Rain? But it's a lovely sunny day!"

"Doesn't matter. She's like a barometer, Nathan always said."

"Nathan?"

"My dad." Ben stopped scratching Elsie and burrowed his hand in her fur for comfort. "He adopted me from the orphanage. He died in the war."

"Oh, rotten luck!"

She didn't say she was sorry, and Ben was glad. He hated it when people said they were sorry, as if that should somehow make things better. It *was* rotten luck that Nathan had been killed, when he wasn't even fighting, *couldn't* fight because of his leg. Rotten luck was *exactly* the right response.

"That's why I live here on my own," he said. "I'm just waiting for my brother to come back. He's been at the war too."

It was the first time he had said this out loud to anyone other than Mercy. He hoped it sounded convincing.

"What about your uncle and aunt?" he asked, to change the subject. "Will they let you keep Federico?"

"They can't stop me," said Lotti, proudly raising her chin. "It's my house, after all."

Even to her own ears it didn't sound convincing. Lotti glanced at her wristwatch. Her dinner was served in the kitchen at seven o'clock sharp, and Aunt Vera hated it when she was late. Today of all days it made sense not to annoy her.

"I have to go," she said regretfully. "Come along, Federico! You can walk a bit, now that you've eaten. You're much heavier than you look. Ben, would you mind awfully checking again that Malachy Campbell isn't lurking?"

The coast was clear. Dogs and children trooped out of the cabin onto the rear deck.

It was approaching the time of day Nathan had loved best, when mist hovered over the water and the sun's sinking rays touched the dirty canal with gold. Ben felt a quiet glow of pride as Lotti caught her breath.

"It's even better from the roof," he offered.

He stepped onto the storage box and hoisted himself lightly onto the roof, then turned and held out his hand. Lotti glanced at her wristwatch, then climbed after him.

"Oh!" she cried. "Oh, you're right."

The sun sank, the shadows lengthened, the gold of the water deepened. Ben and Lotti sat with the dogs between them and forgot about aunts and being late and wars and rotten luck.

It never failed, this magic of the world seen from the roof of the boat.

"When I was little, we used to go on holiday to my grandmother's house in France," said Lotti at last. "Papa kept a little rowing boat in the boathouse by the river. I always thought, when we went out in it, how different everything looks from the water. Like anything is possible, you know? Like you're completely free to go anywhere you want. Is that what it's like living on the *Sparrowhawk*?"

"Yes," said Ben. "That's exactly what it's like. Or it was, when Sam and Nathan were alive."

"Do you know how to drive her?"

"I do, actually." Ben blushed under Lotti's admiring gaze.

"Maybe one day you can teach me." Lotti sighed, then reluctantly stood up. "I really do have to go, but may I come back?"

Ben didn't miss the falter in her voice. She sounded vulnerable suddenly, and much less confident.

"Of course you can," he said. "Just make sure Malachy Campbell doesn't see you."

"I'll try to come back tomorrow, then," said Lotti happily. "And you can show me all over your boat."

She held out her hand. Ben, having shaken it, found that he didn't want to let go.

He stood and watched as Lotti and Federico ran down the towpath, away from town. As they turned onto Barton Lane, he thought how strange it was, that even though she had barely stopped talking throughout her visit, the silence when Lotti had gone was even louder.

Earlier that afternoon, just a hundred yards away from the *Sparrowhawk*, at about the time when Lotti was telling Ben about being expelled from school, Malachy Campbell knocked on the door of the lonely cottage Ben had run past earlier. A thin, untidy young woman rushed to answer the door, her wire-rimmed spectacles slipping down her nose.

"You seen my Chihuahua?" asked Malachy Campbell.

The young woman, whose name was Clara Primrose, pushed her spectacles back into place and regarded him with an air of intense disappointment.

"Showed it to you last week, remember?" said Malachy, conscious that the air of disappointment had changed to one of blazing fury. "He's been nicked."

"Well, he's not here," Clara said, and slammed the door.

≈ ≈ ≈

In the summer of 1914, Clara Primrose had been eighteen, at university and in love with a fellow student called Max. Max wrote poetry and hated fighting and was the last person you could imagine as a soldier, but he had gone into the army as soon as war was declared.

"When it's all over, I'll come for you," he wrote to her, over and again in smuggled letters through those four bleak years. "Promise you'll wait for me!"

Clara promised, and waited. She waited as she finished university, and she waited in the hospital where she volunteered as a nurse, and though she had received no news of him for months, she was still waiting now. Her parents disapproved of Max so much they had kicked her out of their home. She had moved to Great Barton because nobody here knew her, and she had rented the lonely cottage by the canal so that when Max arrived no neighbors would pry on them. She had told her landlady that she was a writer looking for peace and quiet to finish her novel, and the landlady believed her because, as she told Mercy Jenkins in the baker's queue, Clara with her spectacles and the general air she had of falling apart— all that red hair escaping its pins and her sweaters full of holes—well, she *looked* like a writer, didn't she? And though it wasn't exactly proper for a young lady to live all alone like that, everyone knew artists were mad.

It didn't occur to anyone that Clara had a secret.

She hadn't always been like this. At university Clara had been positively curvy, and worn her hair in a rich, swirling curtain down her back, and she had laughed a lot. As a nurse, she had been neat and efficient. But now ...

Well, war and waiting did things to a person.

Really, Clara earned her living as a translator. After Malachy Campbell had gone, she took a pile of papers from the drawer in the kitchen table, made tea, forgot to drink it, picked up a pencil, hunted for a sharpener, found one in the fruit bowl and settled down to work. She tried to concentrate on her translation, which was about fertilizers and agricultural production, but her mind refused to settle. How her heart had leaped when Malachy knocked on the door, thinking ... *hoping*, really ... that it was Max! But then her heart leaped at *every* knock on the door. She pushed aside her translation, picked up a blank sheet of paper and began a letter to Max's mother, then pushed that away too after a few lines, and went out for a walk instead.

Max's mother never answered anyway.

Clara had passed the *Sparrowhawk* many times before and never paid it much attention, but today was different. Today for the first time, she heard voices on board.

She stepped closer, feeling curious, then stopped.

A girl and a boy sat cross-legged side by side with their backs to her on the roof of the boat, two dogs between them in a tangled heap. Clara narrowed her eyes. The larger dog was a black and white spaniel cross. The smaller one ... Clara's mouth formed a silent "Oh!"

The smaller one was Malachy Campbell's stolen Chihuahua.

Probably, Clara should have said something.

A stolen dog!

But Clara disliked Malachy Campbell, and she didn't approve of keeping dogs in cages. And also, there was the light on the water, the mist, the peacefulness ... To Clara's eyes, in that moment, the children and dogs on the boat seemed to belong to a different world, an enchanted place like a fairy tale, or poetry.

Tomorrow, maybe, if they were still here, she would return and introduce herself. But right now Clara tiptoed away, carefully, so as not to disturb the feeling she'd not had for a very long time, that anything was possible.

Chapter Three

If you could hug yourself while you run, Lotti would be doing it as she ran home through the woods up Barton Lane.

After the awful loneliness of school, two new friends! In one day!

Granted, neither had had any choice in the matter. She had stolen one and broken into the home of the other. Nonetheless, she felt giddy with the joy of it.

The lane began to climb. Lotti stopped running to catch her breath and felt a stab of panic as Federico raced ahead.

What if he carried on running and didn't come back?

What if he wasn't her friend at all? What if . . .

Yip! Yip! Yip!

Federico hurtled back down the lane, straight into her arms.

"I'll never leave you!" he seemed to tell her with his ecstatic, wriggling body.

"Never, never, never!" Lotti replied, hugging him close.

The woods gave way to open hillside. This had been a favorite walk when Lotti's parents were alive. Together, Lotti, Théophile and Isobel had crunched through winter snow, lingered in spring's flowering gorse, lain in the summer grass to listen to the skylarks sing. On the way home, if Lotti was tired, Papa had carried her on his back, snorting and pawing the ground like a pony. Lotti loved every tree, every stone, every curve of the hills surrounding Barton Lacey, but there was no time to stop and look at them. If she was to be back in time for supper, neat and tidy as her aunt liked, she would have to hurry.

And yet her footsteps dragged.

"They can't stop me keeping him," she had said to Ben, and for as long as she was planning to rescue Federico, Lotti had pretended to herself that this was true because she wanted very much to save him. But the closer she got to home, the less realistic this seemed. Papa would have celebrated Federico's rescue.

He *loved* animals. And Mama would have been pleased too, because she hated any form of cruelty. But Uncle Hubert and Aunt Vera?

It wouldn't do, Lotti thought, to barge in with Federico. She must choose her moment, and also think of a story that didn't involve actual *stealing*. Lotti viewed her kidnap of Federico more as liberation than theft, but Uncle Hubert and Aunt Vera probably wouldn't see it that way ...

"I'm going to have to hide you for a bit," she told Federico. "But where?"

Federico licked her hand.

They cleared the brow of the hill and Barton Lacey came into view, a square honey-colored house nestled in gardens and trees. As Lotti and Federico began their descent toward it, a light flickered at the eastern perimeter gate. Lotti's heart leaped.

She knew what that light was—Zachy, out smoking his evening pipe!

Zachy, whose crowbar she had stolen ... Zachy, who used to scold her for picking fruit before it was ripe but always saved her the best strawberries, who let her trot after him with her own little trowel to dig in bedding plants, who had adored Mama and known Lotti since she was a baby ...

Zachy, who lived in a cottage right on the edge of the Barton grounds, where her uncle and aunt never went ... who actively disliked the Netherburys—Zachy would help!

Lotti, with Federico at her heels, raced down the hill toward the light.

Zachy *was* a darling, just as she had told Ben. His ancient face, white-whiskered and wrinkled like a walnut, had broken into a grin at the sight of Lotti and Federico, and he and the little dog had taken to each other at once. Lotti left Federico nestled in a crate in front of the fire in Zachy's cottage, with the old gardener preparing him bread and milk.

"I just have to explain about him to Uncle and Aunt," she had told Zachy, who had grunted like he was saying *good luck with that*. But now it was very nearly seven o'clock and Sally, the only indoor servant left at Barton since the war, would be dishing up Lotti's supper.

The rain predicted by Elsie began to fall as she came out of Zachy's cottage. By the time she had run through the grounds—the kitchen garden and the orchard, the beech alley where Papa had taught her to ride, the glade where Mama had loved to read, the stream, the bridge, the elegant main lawn—she was drenched. Quiet as a mouse, she slipped into the scullery. Perhaps, if she could just tiptoe along the servants' corridor then up to her room to change her clothes and brush her hair before stealing back down to the kitchen ... Like Zachy, Sally was fond of Lotti and disliked her employers. She only stayed at Barton because she was saving up to buy a pub with her fiancé near her home in Kent, now that he was home from the war. Sally would cover for her ...

"Charlotte?"

Hubert Netherbury's voice called out from the drawing room as Lotti reached the stairs. Lotti froze.

"In here, Charlotte, please."

And perhaps, if Lotti was suitably apologetic, Uncle Hubert would not be so very angry that she was late ... perhaps Aunt Vera would not notice Lotti's sodden clothes, the tear in her sailor suit, her hair wild from the wind and rain ...

Lotti walked slowly toward the drawing room.

Hubert Netherbury sat in Papa's chair by the fire, a glass of sherry in his hand. One glance at his thin, pressed mouth told Lotti that he *was* furious, but he said nothing, didn't even look at her, just waited for her to stammer an excuse.

"I was out walking." Lotti stared at the carpet as she spoke, and how surprised Ben would have been to see her now—Lotti the dog rescuer, the housebreaker, barely able to speak!

This was what she hated most about her uncle, how *small* he made her feel.

"I'm sorry I'm late, I lost track of time."

"Charlotte, your *clothes* ..." Vera Netherbury spoke in a hushed, reproachful voice, as if the sight of Lotti gave her physical pain. "Your hair ..."

Lotti glanced up at her aunt and flushed with rage. She was wearing one of Mama's favorite shawls, an extravagant blue cashmere embroidered with butterflies with a deep silk fringe. On lovely Isobel St. Rémy, it had looked beautiful. On mean Vera Netherbury, it was hateful and absurd.

"I got caught in the rain," muttered Lotti, failing to sound apologetic.

Hubert Netherbury toyed with his sherry glass, then very delicately put it down and flexed his hand. Lotti, remembering the slap at Great Barton station, flinched and looked at the carpet again.

"Be very careful, Charlotte," said her uncle softly. "Or I may change my mind about not sending you away to school."

"I'm sorry, Uncle," whispered Lotti. "I won't be late again."

"No, you won't. Now get out of my sight."

Lotti fled.

Up in her room, Lotti threw herself on the bed and punched the mattress. How did her uncle make her feel like this, so wretched, with so few words? She had been wrong, so wrong, to come home! She should have stayed at school! Except ... the lovely hills around Barton Lacey, the memories of Mama and Papa ... and now the *Sparrowhawk*, and Ben, and most of all Federico. Federico, who was now her responsibility, who she had already let down by appearing as such a disheveled mess before her uncle and aunt ... what would happen to him if she was sent away to school? Who would look after him?

Moune. The thought came from nowhere, but that was hopeless of course, because as well as Moune being far away in France, there was the awful and terrible fact of her silence ...

Oh, what should she do?

The door opened and Sally came in, carrying a basin.

"Out of those clothes now, young lady, while I build up the fire," she said briskly. "I've brought you hot water for a good wash, then his *lordship* says you're to go straight to bed. *No supper*, his *lordship* says. Well, no fear, *I* say. *I've* no time to look after a sick child, not while I run this place single-handed because he's too mean to pay for staff. And sick is exactly what you'll be if you don't get warm and fed. Come on, Lots, chop chop. Clean up, and I'll go and fetch the food. Ow! Ow! What are you doing, you mad child?"

Lotti had flung her arms round Sally's waist. Just for a moment, the maid's face softened as she hugged her back. Sally had witnessed the slap at the station, and comforted Lotti afterward, and then written a strong letter to her fiancé telling him what a shame it was that Hubert Netherbury had been too old to go to the war and die there.

"Don't you worry, Lots," she said. "Life'll work out. It always does in the end."

An hour later, scrubbed clean and full of boiled eggs, toast, and prunes and custard, lying in bed with a fire in the grate and a hot brick at her feet, Lotti was feeling better.

Of course she was right to have come home! The way the little dog had run into her arms in the woods, the feel of his warm body wriggling against hers as she hugged him! With the brief exception of Queen Victoria the cat, who was now dead, Moune, who was gone, and

Sally, who would soon be leaving, Lotti hadn't hugged anyone since her parents died.

How *good* it had felt to hug Federico. How completely, absolutely *right*.

And Federico wasn't the only thing that had felt right today. Lotti thought of the *Sparrowhawk*, of sitting with Ben and Elsie and Federico, watching the evening light. It was so simple, but it was all she wanted. To feel peaceful and wanted. With *friends*.

To belong.

Life always worked out, Sally had said. Well, Sally was often right, but sometimes life needed help. What Lotti must do now was not get sent back to school, which meant behaving absolutely and completely impeccably before her uncle and aunt. She could do that! From now on, she would be a model of Usefulness. She wouldn't give her uncle and aunt the slightest reason to be displeased and soon—when the moment was right—she would explain about Federico in a way that meant she could keep him . . .

Meanwhile, tomorrow afternoon, careful not to be seen, she and Federico would return to the *Sparrowhawk* . . .

On the *Sparrowhawk* Ben, like Lotti, was in bed. Unlike Lotti he was hungry.

He had tried to heat a can of soup for his supper, but both the stove in the galley and the one in Nathan's workshop smoked, and he hadn't been able to light a fire. In the end, he had eaten the soup cold but abandoned it after a few mouthfuls. Now he lay in his berth under all the blankets he could find, cuddled up to Elsie for extra warmth, his mind whirring.

The *Sparrowhawk* was in a worse state than he had thought. She didn't just need a scrub and a lick of paint. All her windows needed recaulking, her metalwork was spotted with rust, and he hadn't even dared to inspect the engine. How much was it going to cost to put all this right?

"First thing in the morning," he told Elsie, "I'll go and look for a job."

He'd ask at the boatyard, where he'd done odd jobs since living with Mercy, running errands and messages. John Snell, who ran it, had known Nathan; the two men had liked each other. And he could advise Ben on the *Sparrowhawk* too, where to start with getting her back into shape, ready for when Sam came home.

When Sam came home ...

The truth was, Ben had no idea when his brother would return. He had lied to Mercy, and now he had lied to Lotti too, which had been more difficult because there was something about Lotti that made him want to be honest with her. But a secret was a secret, and this one was not for sharing. There had been no letter from the War Office and if the constable Albert Skinner found out, Ben would be taken into care again and separated from Elsie. The *Sparrowhawk*, he imagined, would either be sold or left to rot.

How long could he keep up the pretense before anyone found out?

Chapter Four

The next morning at dawn, Lotti stole out to take Federico for a quick run on the hills, then returned the little dog to Zachy. After breakfast, which she ate in the kitchen, she sewed for four hours, irreproachably dressed in a scratchy navy pinafore, her curls pulled into neat braids. With a tremendous exercise of will, she managed to hide her impatience, but as soon as her aunt dismissed her, she sneaked away to fetch Federico and ran down to the *Sparrowhawk*.

Oh, please let Ben be happy to see me, she thought as she ran. Please let it be as lovely as I remember it!

John Snell had agreed to take Ben on at the boatyard, six mornings a week from eight to one o'clock, in return for half the pay of an adult, permission to bring Elsie with him, and no questions asked about his living arrangements. Ben had spent the morning cleaning the darkest corners of a crumbling boathouse, untouched since the beginning of the war. Now he wanted to get to work on his boat, but the task was daunting. Lotti found him standing on the towpath with Elsie, examining the *Sparrowhawk*'s paintwork.

It is one thing to meet under extreme circumstances, when one person is running away and another person is hiding her, and there is the excitement of a stolen dog and a homecoming. It is quite another to meet in the cold light of day. For a moment, neither Lotti nor Ben knew what to say. But the dogs had no such difficulty, and it is impossible to remain awkward when you have two dogs leaping after each other around you, barking wildly. In fact, it's impossible not to laugh. And in the end, all Lotti needed to say was, "I came back." And all Ben needed to say was, "Shall I show you the *Sparrowhawk*, then?"

On board, with the dogs cavorting around her, Lotti inspected the cabin, taking in all the things that in the commotion of yesterday she had not noticed. There was the damp, the cold, the draft from the windows, but also all of Nathan's lovely, useful details—the drawers under the berths, the fold-down table and the chairs hanging on the wall beside it, the little galley where three tin mugs hung from hooks over the sink. Best of all were the pictures, painted straight onto the walls, a new one for each of the boys' birthdays—birds peeping out among trees, dogs running on a towpath, a black and white cat sleeping behind the stove.

"I love it," she said. "It's wonderful."

"She needs a lot of work."

"I can help!" Again, Ben heard that slight falter in Lotti's voice, a loss of confidence, like she was afraid he would say no. But Ben didn't want to say no. He had felt so alone, for so long . . .

All afternoon, watched by the dogs curled together on Ben's berth, Ben and Lotti polished and swept and cleaned and dusted until the living quarters of the *Sparrowhawk* gleamed. They threw open the doors and windows to chase out the damp, they flapped sheets and blankets in the sunshine to air them. Ben cleared the stoves' flue pipes and at last managed to light a fire.

He boiled water in the kettle and made toast, Lotti unfolded the table and together they sat down to eat.

"To the *Sparrowhawk*!" said Lotti, raising her mug.

"To the *Sparrowhawk*!" responded Ben.

They clinked mugs. The dogs barked in response. Ben and Lotti both laughed, and began to talk about how tomorrow, if the weather was fine, they would begin to sand down the external wood in preparation for painting. When Lotti and Federico left the *Sparrowhawk*, both she and Ben felt the same warm glow, which came from the knowledge that they had found a true friend and also that maybe their separate plans—to keep Federico, to stay at Barton Lacey, to remain on the *Sparrowhawk*—were going to work.

For one glorious week, nobody bothered them.

Then the policeman came.

Albert Skinner was not a heroic kind of policeman. He was small and tubby, with pigeon feet that made his bottom stick out, and for the past three years there had been about his shoulders a rather defeated slouch. Pub landlords breaking up fights seldom called for him to help, and children laughed when he tried to move them on from places where they shouldn't be. Yet for all this, he was not undignified.

And he was conscientious. Stubborn as a terrier, his colleagues said. He had a reputation, once he was on a case, of never giving up.

For the past week, Albert had watched the *Sparrowhawk* from afar, believing that what Mercy had told him was true and that Sam would soon return to Great Barton. But with the passing days, he had grown increasingly troubled. If this went on much longer, he would write to the War Office himself for the exact date of Sam's return. Meanwhile, Ben's lifestyle was neither appropriate, nor strictly legal. A week exactly after Lotti and Ben's first meeting, he set off to the *Sparrowhawk* to tell him so.

There is something about seeing a policeman, when you have a secret, which induces an immediate sense of guilt. Ben saw Albert Skinner first. He was on the rear deck, priming the sanded doors, and the moment he saw him Ben was filled with the absolute certainty that Albert knew he had lied about the letter from the War Office and was coming to carry him off to the orphanage.

Lotti, who was sanding the roof, caught Ben's gasp, followed his line of vision and immediately assumed that Albert Skinner had come to arrest her for stealing Federico, currently asleep with Elsie in Nathan's workshop but liable to wake up at any moment and give the whole game away. In fact, she had been right when she told Ben that Malachy Campbell wasn't the sort of person to go to the police. Albert Skinner wasn't in the least bit interested in Federico. But Lotti had no way of knowing this, and she braced herself for the worst.

Albert approached. Lotti and Ben assumed wholly unconvincing expressions of innocence.

"Good afternoon," said Albert, who liked to be civil even when imparting bad news.

"Good afternoon," they muttered, and in his mind Ben saw the *Sparrowhawk* in the hands of a stranger, Elsie in a dog pound, the metal beds of an orphanage dormitory, while Lotti felt her uncle's slap and imagined Federico in chains . . .

"I have come to ask you," said Albert Skinner, "why you are not in school."

Later he would remember this moment, when Lotti and Ben's expressions changed from guilt to relief, before descending into protest. He would tell himself that that was the moment when he should have known they were a force to be reckoned with. But the relief, though enormous, was only fleeting and very quickly gave way to a level of protest he had not expected.

"What do you mean, *school?*" Lotti cried.

If Albert was startled by Lotti's appearance, barefoot and dressed in a pair of rolled-up overalls stolen from Aunt Vera's jumble pile, he did not let it distract him. "School means school," he said. "I don't know how else to put it. Everyone knows what school is. Children go to it to learn, until they are fourteen. I am telling you about it because it's the law."

"You're wrong," said Lotti. "School ends when you're twelve. My uncle specifically told me so."

"It's a *new* law," said Albert. "And I am never wrong."

"But that's a *terrible* law!"

Albert was conscious, as so many people were on first meeting Lotti, of an incipient headache.

"It doesn't matter if you think the law is terrible," he said. "You can't change it. I am just here to tell you . . ."

He paused. Federico, hearing Lotti's agitation, was howling in sympathy from Nathan's workshop.

"What is that?" asked Albert.

"It's nothing," said Lotti. "I mean, it's a dog. My dog. He's ill."

"Do you want to go to him?"

"Not really."

"Right." Albert hesitated. "Well, as I was saying . . ."

"I can't go to school." Ben, who had been staring at Albert in shocked silence, finally spoke. "I have a job. I need the money. I have to repair the *Sparrowhawk*. For when my brother gets back," he added quickly.

"About that," said Albert. "I was wondering when . . ."

"I can't go to school either," Lotti cut in firmly. "For many reasons, not least because school is hateful. It's all very well for the government to make these laws, but they don't have to *live* them."

"I'm afraid I'll have to talk to your parents about that," said Albert.

"They're dead," snapped Lotti, and was savagely pleased to see Albert flush.

Ben had been thinking hard. "Clara would have said if I had to go to school."

"Who," asked Lotti, "is Clara?"

"She's my neighbor. She lives in the cottage over there, and she came to introduce herself the evening after I moved in. She's a writer. She would know about school, and she never said a thing about it. Quite the contrary. I told her I was working in the boatyard, and she said that must be nice, and how boats were like fairy tales, or poetry, or something."

"Well, let's ask her, then," said Lotti.

"It won't make a slightest difference," said Albert, but it was too late. Lotti had slithered off the roof onto the towpath and was marching away toward Clara Primrose's cottage.

Ben jumped off the rear deck and went after her. All Albert could do was follow.

Chapter Five

Clara was confused. All these months living in solitude, and suddenly her little front garden was crowded with people she hadn't invited, all talking at the same time; her neighbor Ben and a policeman, and the girl who was always hanging around the *Sparrowhawk*, who had stolen the Chihuahua. Clara didn't want them here, but how could she get rid of them? In the background, she heard the five o'clock train whistle as it pulled into the station. She had a sudden vision of Max on the train, Max walking from the station, Max arriving while all these people were here quarreling, when she had waited for him all this time in perfect isolation. Perhaps if she cried they might go away. But Clara, in her former life as a student, had agreed with her friend Kitty that women who cried to get what they wanted were despicable.

"Better to be very, very haughty," Kitty had said.

Clara pushed her glasses back up her nose.

"I have no idea what you are all doing here," she announced, as grandly as you can in a sweater worn back to front, and a moth-eaten one at that. "But I'd be much obliged if you would leave."

Albert, shouting above Lotti in a not very dignified attempt to be heard, informed her that children had to go to school.

"But what does that have to do with me?" asked Clara.

"Nothing," said Albert, whose headache was getting worse.

"Tell him the law's wrong," ordered Lotti.

"What law?"

"The law that says they have to remain in education until they are fourteen," grumbled Albert Skinner.

"Is there such a law?"

"You see?" Albert turned to Lotti. "She doesn't know."

He felt triumphant, and at the same time also a little ashamed of being so pleased at having proved a child wrong, but both feelings turned to aggravation as he realized Lotti didn't look the least bit defeated.

"*Remain in education until they're fourteen,*" she repeated. "That is what you said, isn't it?"

Albert wrinkled his brow. She was up to something, he could tell, but what?

"What I mean," Lotti continued, "is could someone educate us at home? Or at their home? Or even on a boat? Someone who knew what they were doing, like a tutor?"

"I suppose they could, yes."

"Someone like Miss Clara, who is a writer and so must be very educated?"

Ben gazed at Lotti in wonder. Clara Primrose stared at her aghast. Albert Skinner scratched his head.

"Someone like Miss Clara. Yes, I suppose she could."

"But I don't want to be a teacher!" protested Clara.

Lotti turned to face her. Albert, foreseeing another battle, decided to beat a retreat while his dignity was still salvageable, and announced that he would return soon.

As he walked away, he was conscious of an uncomfortable feeling that he had been outplayed.

When it came to Ben and Lotti, it was a feeling he was going to have to get used to.

The little crowd, minus Albert but including the dogs whom Ben had let out of the *Sparrowhawk*, were making their way into the cottage, and Clara was feeling even more confused.

"I don't want to be a teacher," she repeated. "I'm a

writer. I need peace, quiet. I need solitude. I want you to go."

Ben, never one to willingly cause trouble, glanced uneasily at Lotti. Lotti, unconcerned, bounced on one of the two sagging armchairs by the fire.

"You have a *lot* of books." She picked up a volume of poetry from the floor and spelled out the author's name. " G-O-E-T-H-E. Goaty! Goat?"

"It's pronounced G-E-R-T-E-R. It's poetry. It's German."

"*German?*" Ben was outraged.

"I didn't know Germans *had* poetry," said Lotti.

"Well, they do, beautiful poetry." Clara flushed, and resisted the urge to throw a book at Lotti's head.

"But *why* are you reading *German* poetry?" demanded Ben. "When we have just fought a war against them?"

"Poetry has no frontiers," Clara informed him frostily.

Ben sniffed, unconvinced. Lotti put down the Goethe and picked up another volume. "Is this one German too? Look, it's got your name in the title. *Für Clara*. For Clara?"

"Give me that!" Clara snatched the book from Lotti's hand.

"You should tell my uncle about Germans and poetry. He thinks all foreigners are savages. Including me, because I'm half French. Will you teach us German poetry?"

"*Not* German," said Ben decisively.

"Not *anything*!" cried Clara.

"But it's the perfect solution!" said Lotti.

"Solution to what?" asked Clara, practically shrieking.

"Your uncle would never let you have lessons with me anyway," said Ben, ignoring Clara. "He's too posh."

"He's mean though too, and I bet Miss Clara wouldn't cost as much as school. No offense, Miss Clara."

The clock on the mantelpiece chimed the half hour, and Clara felt suddenly exhausted. It took ten minutes to walk here from the station, twenty at the most if the bridge was open and you had to go the long way. Max wasn't going to come tonight. She sank into the armchair opposite Lotti's and closed her eyes.

"Perfect solution to what?" she asked.

"Ben has his job," explained Lotti. "And I have a problem with my dog Federico."

"The dog you have stolen." Clara opened her eyes and, seeing Lotti's expression of terror, felt sorry that she had spoken. "Don't worry, I won't say anything."

"The thing is," said Lotti, sounding more subdued, "when my uncle hears about this law, he'll send me away. He's much too much of a snob to let me go to the Barton school. So you see, a tutor's the only way. It's worth a try. Honestly, even if it weren't for Federico, I couldn't bear boarding school again."

"They shut her in the coal cellar," said Ben. "All night."

Clara, remembering her own miserable school days, pressed her lips together.

"Will you teach us?" All of Lotti's bravado was gone now, and she was almost pleading. "I promise I'll be good. I *would* actually *like* to learn. I had this idea yesterday that I could be an animal doctor. I took a thorn out of Federico's foot and he looked at me with these big, grateful eyes—he has such beautiful eyes— and I thought *imagine doing this all the time*! I'd need a proper education for that, wouldn't I? What would you like to be, Ben, if you had time for an education and you could be or do anything you wanted? Like Miss Clara being a writer and me being an animal doctor, what would you . . ."

"I'd build bridges." The answer came from nowhere, but as soon as he said it Ben knew it was true. "And boats. Like Mr. Brunel, the engineer. Nathan took us to Bristol once, to see the suspension bridge he built there over the gorge, and it was . . ."

He trailed off. Words couldn't do justice to how Ben had felt, the first time he saw Mr. Brunel's bridge suspended two hundred and forty-five feet above the Clifton gorge.

Lotti smiled. "That would be a good thing for you, Ben."

A moment's quiet settled over the room, and Clara was reminded of the first time she had seen these two, sitting together on the roof of the *Sparrowhawk*, and the feeling she had had then that anything was possible. Max would like these two, she thought. I like them.

"All right," she said. "I'll do it."

Chapter Six

It was the morning after the encounter with Clara and Albert Skinner. Hubert Netherbury sat in Lotti's papa's chair in the Barton Lacey study, a map spread out before him on the desk. His face, as he observed his niece standing on the fine Persian rug before him, was irritated. His wife had informed him at breakfast that Lady Clarion went to Scotland every year, and couldn't believe the Netherburys had never been. Hubert must plan a holiday immediately, Vera had said, and never mind the cost. He had been in the middle of doing this when Lotti knocked on the door, and he did not like to be interrupted.

"I don't understand what you need a tutor *for*," he grumbled, when she had explained what she wanted.

Lotti, quaking inside, couldn't quite meet her uncle's eye, but she did manage to keep her voice steady.

"To teach me," she said. "And also, because of the law."

"What law?"

Lotti had prepared her story in advance. All she needed now was the courage to tell it.

"There's this lady I met at the library . . ."

"What lady?"

"A tutor."

"A *female* tutor?" Hubert Netherbury looked appalled.

"I went to the library to change my book," Lotti plowed on. "It was a Dickens novel, *Oliver Twist*, and the tutor likes Dickens too so she asked had I read *Great Expectations*, and I said yes, we read it at school, and *she* said oh what school is that, then? And *I* said it *used* to be St. Margaret's Academy for Girls but I had to leave, and *she* said where do you go now and *I* said I was Making Myself Useful at Home and *she* said, but how old are you, my dear? Don't you know that a new law was introduced last year which says you must be in education until you are fourteen?"

Uncle Hubert made a spluttering sound. Lotti secretly began to enjoy herself.

"I said *no*, I must tell my uncle and aunt! But I'm

afraid they won't want me to go away again because I am So *Very* Useful to My Aunt, and then *she* said well I am busy in the mornings but if your aunt can spare you in the afternoons *I* can give you lessons and prepare you for the School Certificate—apparently, this is quite an acceptable alternative to school—and of course much, *much* cheaper—and so *I* said . . ."

"Enough!" howled Uncle Hubert.

"He said yes!" yelled Lotti, running toward the *Sparrowhawk* that afternoon. "Ben, my uncle said yes! I can learn with you and Clara! I don't have to go away to school!" Lotti twirled, flapping the skirt of her mended sailor suit, then drew a squashed wax-paper packet from her satchel. "I convinced him! Me! Uncle Hubert! Put the kettle on, Sally gave me cake!"

They drank their tea side by side on the tiny foredeck, legs dangling over the water.

"How d'you convince him, then?" asked Ben.

"Just told him the truth." Lotti grinned and broke a piece of cake in two for the dogs.

"Lotti!"

"All right, maybe not the *exact* truth. I didn't mention Constable Skinner, or you. And he hasn't *completely* agreed. He wants to meet Clara—we'll have to make sure she looks respectable—and if he likes her, he's agreed to a trial period. He and Aunt Vera are going on some ghastly holiday to Scotland at the end of May. I've got until then to show him I can be good. Actually, not good. I have to be *exemplary*." Lotti puffed out her chest, curling her lip in imitation of her uncle : "*And I mean EXEMPLARY, young lady, or I shall send you away to a school where they whip you with stinging nettles before breakfast and the only food is cold worm porridge.*'

Ben began to laugh. Lotti shoved him with her shoulder.

"Come on, let's go and tell Miss Clara!"

Two days later, Clara, dressed in a pre-war suit and stockings that almost matched, went for her interview at Barton Lacey, where she passed Hubert Netherbury's respectability test. Hubert Netherbury offered her shockingly low wages, which she accepted because she felt sorry for his niece.

Everybody enjoyed the first lesson with Clara, including Clara herself. Its content was determined by what books she had found in the public library, its structure involved a great deal of student participation and its general atmosphere was one of loud, talkative chaos.

"Here is a book about British kings and queens,"

Clara informed them when they arrived at her cottage. "Please read it."

"But it's huge," Ben protested.

"I'm sure you will rise to the challenge."

"And there's two of us and only one book."

"You read the first half, and I'll read the second," Lotti suggested. "And we can tell each other what happens."

"Excellent problem-solving, Lotti!" said Clara. "Now, here is a famous French poem. It's one of my favorites. It's about rain falling on the rooftops of a town, and the poet feels like it's raining in his heart."

"It sounds miserable," said Ben.

"It's actually rather beautiful," Lotti told him. "Papa used to recite it whenever it rained."

"Good, Lotti, then you can teach it to Ben. Right, I also found a book about the digestive system of cows. You'll need to know about these things, if you want to be a vet. I thought you could copy out these diagrams. And look, Ben, here's a book on famous bridges. You copy those. And then I suppose we'd better do some mathematics, although I'm not so good at mathematics."

"I am," said Ben.

"That's wonderful!" Clara looked relieved. "*Nil desperandum*, as Sister used to say at the hospital—do not despair! Oh, lordy, we have to do Latin too . . ."

"We did loads of Latin at St. Margaret's, miss."

"Lotti, *please* call me Clara! Miss makes me sound ancient, and I'm only twenty-three."

"We did loads of Latin at St. Margaret's, *Clara*. I'm actually really good at it. *I* can teach it!"

The class had been, Clara said with a smile as she let them out just before the five o'clock train, extremely democratic.

"Which is a word derived from the Ancient Greek— *demos*, meaning the common people, and *kratos*, meaning rule."

"Meaning," Lotti expanded joyfully when she and Ben parted at the *Sparrowhawk*, "that *we* are in charge! And did you notice, Ben, how pretty Clara looked when she smiled? Almost like she was really young!"

Yes, everyone enjoyed lessons with Clara, and over the next few weeks it seemed that this new way of life might last. Ben and Lotti worked hard at their lessons, at the boatyard, at Being Useful and Exemplary, at repairing the *Sparrowhawk*. Clara, busy and no longer lonely, smiled more and more often. Federico put on weight and his coat grew glossy. Elsie, for reasons no one could understand, took to sleeping most of the day.

Soon, Lotti told herself, she would explain to her aunt and uncle about Federico. It wasn't fair to keep him hidden away. She rose at dawn to walk him before the Netherburys woke, and she gave him a good run in the afternoon, but he spent the rest of his days when Zachy was working tied up behind the gardener's cottage, which was no life for a sociable dog. To be fair, she had *tried* to tell her uncle. On two occasions, she had gathered up the courage to knock on the door of the study. Each time, when Hubert Netherbury bade her enter, Lotti's eyes drifted to his hand, flexing and unflexing, and she lost her nerve.

Soon, soon, soon ... but not yet.

"Soon" was also Ben's reply to Albert Skinner, each time the policeman returned to the *Sparrowhawk*. Once he heard that Clara would be tutoring Ben and Lotti, Albert had said no more about school, but on the subject of Sam he was relentless.

"Any news?" he asked, at least once a week.

"Not long now," Ben would reply, buying time.

Soon, soon, soon ...

The days lengthened, bluebells flooded the woods. Under normal circumstances, Lotti would have loved to drift among them, as she used to with her parents. Papa had adored bluebells, the way the flowers hovered over the forest floor like a secret blue sea. "Where shall we sail to on this ocean of blue?" he would say on their walks, and together he and Lotti and Mama would stay out late into the evenings, breathing in the sweet hyacinth scent and making up adventures.

But these were not normal circumstances and there was never time to linger.

Under the surface, secrets bubbled.

And sooner or later, all secrets bubble over.

Chapter Seven

On the day before the Netherbury's Scottish holiday, Aunt Vera held a Women's Institute fête committee coffee morning. Included in the meeting was to be Lady Clarion, whom Aunt Vera was so very anxious to impress.

Lotti was to Be Useful, handing round sandwiches.

She rose feeling optimistic. It was the last day of Clara's probation period: soon, the threat of boarding school would be gone for ever and from tomorrow, for almost a whole week, she would have Barton to herself. When the Netherburys returned, happy and relaxed from their holiday, she would introduce them to Federico.

Almost definitely.

For now, she just needed one more day of Exemplary behavior.

Lotti took no chances. She got up earlier than usual for Federico's morning walk, she kept him on the lead in case he went anywhere he shouldn't, she stayed out only half their usual time in case her aunt or uncle also rose early. It was just unfortunate that in her hurry to return to the house, as she tied Federico up behind Zachy's cottage, she did not notice how very frayed his rope had become ...

Back in her room, Lotti dressed uncomplainingly in a stiff, old-fashioned sailor suit chosen by her aunt, braided her hair and washed her face until it shone. When she went down for breakfast, Aunt Vera looked at her almost approvingly.

The weather was glorious, Barton Lacey beautiful. The French windows in the drawing room were open to let in the scent of stocks and lilies. The committee ladies began to arrive, and Aunt Vera puffed with pride as they complimented her on her beautiful home. Lotti bit her tongue and picked up the sandwich tray.

"You are a credit to your aunt," Lady Clarion informed her.

Lotti dropped an exemplary curtsey. Aunt Vera simpered.

Everything was going splendidly.

But Federico was growing restless.

For eight weeks, since he had first been tied up behind Zachy's cottage, he had been working on a plan to be free. The plan was simple—he was a simple dog—but it was good.

Federico was chewing through his rope.

How much he chewed depended on how bored he was. Today, after his shortened walk, he was very bored indeed.

And so he chewed, and chewed.

At about the time Lotti started to hand around the sandwiches, the last frayed strand of rope snapped. Federico bounded away from the cottage, streaked silently past Zachy working in the fruit frames, and fled in search of Lotti.

Down through the beech alley where Lotti's papa had taught her to ride, past Lotti's Mama's secret reading spot, over the little bridge. He stopped to relieve himself on the elegant lawn, dug a hole, rolled in it, leaped into the stream, vigorously shook off the water then, remembering his original intention, set off again.

He was thirty feet from the French windows when the pheasant caught his eye.

Federico was fast. The pheasant, unused to predators in the calm grounds of Barton Lacey, was unprepared. Federico approached at a gallop. By the time the pheasant took off in a great beating of wings, the little dog was snapping at its tail feathers.

The pheasant lost its balance. Federico leaped. The pheasant screamed. Federico's jaws snapped shut around its neck.

His entrance to the drawing room was spectacular. Several ladies shrieked. The vicar's wife—a practical person—tried to remove the pheasant from the dog's jaws. Federico refused to let it go. Aunt Vera turned poppy-red, then the color of dirty snow.

Lotti froze.

Delicately, gracefully, as though offering a great gift, Federico deposited the dead pheasant at her feet then sat back and wagged his tail.

Yip?

"Well, I never!" Lady Clarion exclaimed. "If that isn't Malachy Campbell's Chihuahua!"

Chapter Eight

Aunt Vera screamed for her husband. The committee ladies all left, but not before Lady Clarion had explained how Malachy Campbell had once tried to sell her this very dog—it had been thinner then, to be sure, but she would know it anywhere by its ears! Now Lotti hunched by the French windows clutching a trembling Federico as she tried to explain herself to her incandescent uncle and distraught aunt.

"I didn't steal him, I rescued him," she insisted. "It was so cruel, the way Mr. Campbell was keeping him. Someone had to do something . . ."

"Do something?" thundered Uncle Hubert. "*I'll show you something!* I am going to call the police."

He strode out into the hall where the telephone was

kept. There was a brief, shouted conversation, then he marched back in again.

"I spoke to that constable, Albert Skinner," he raged to his wife. "He says no one's reported the dog's theft; says this Campbell character's a well-known crook and probably stole the dog in the first place. Then when I ordered him to fetch the creature himself, he had the nerve to tell me he's off on leave! *Someone can come up from the dog pound tomorrow,* he said. So now"—he glared at Lotti—"on top of harboring an actual thief, we have to shelter the little brute as well."

He lunged forward and seized Federico by the scruff of the neck. The little dog tried to howl but his throat was pulled too tight and he choked.

"You're hurting him!"

Lotti forgot that she was afraid of her uncle. Still holding Federico by the neck, Hubert Netherbury marched out of the drawing room down the servants' corridor to the scullery, roaring for Sally to open up the coal cellar. Pulling, punching, kicking, Lotti fought him every step of the way. Again and again he pushed her aside. Again and again she returned to fight.

But she was so much smaller than her uncle. Sally, tight-lipped, opened the door to the coal cellar. Lotti tried to bar the way, but Hubert Netherbury pushed her out of the way with one hand and threw Federico downstairs as if neither weighed more than a feather.

Then he turned to his niece.

This time, when he slapped her, Lotti saw stars.

Her head was still spinning when he grabbed her by the hair and dragged her back along the corridor and up the stairs to her room.

"Savage!" he thundered, as he flung her inside.

He slammed the door behind her and locked it.

"Let me out!" screamed Lotti. "This is *my* house! You can't lock me in!"

"I can do what I damn well want until you're twenty-one!" her uncle bellowed back. "You'll stay in there until I can find a school desperate enough to take you!"

Lotti kicked the door.

"I won't go to school! And I won't let you send Federico to the pound!"

And then Lotti's blood froze as her uncle began to laugh. "Oh, there's no fear of that," said Hubert Netherbury, and somehow it was more frightening when he spoke softly than when he shouted. "The pound's much too good for the little brute. I'll arrange for him to be shot instead."

Sally came up later with a tray of food and found Lotti sitting on the floor with her back against the wall.

"I'm not hungry." Lotti's voice was hoarse from screaming, her face puffy from crying.

Sally put the tray down and joined Lotti on the floor. "Want a hug?"

Lotti nodded and began to cry again. They sat quietly for a while with Sally's broad arms wrapped round Lotti's slight frame, until at last her sobs subsided and they were able to talk.

"I got news," said Sally. "You ready to hear it?"

Lotti sniffed.

"Your uncle's found a school that'll take you," said Sally. "It's called St. Winifred's Academy for Girls, and it's in Pembrokeshire. Lady Clarion recommended it, so you can imagine what your aunt's like, all *thank you, your gracious ladyship,* etc. Snob. You're to leave on Sunday, the day after tomorrow. I'm to see you on to the train. I'm sorry, Lots. I know it's the last thing you wanted."

Strange, thought Lotti, how she didn't even care. Her uncle could send her to the planet Mars for all the difference it would make. Only one thing mattered now.

"And Federico?"

"Oh, Lots." Sally's arm tightened round Lotti's shoulders. "I'm sorry, sweetheart. A lad's coming from Home Farm tomorrow to put him down, before your uncle and aunt leave for Scotland."

So that was that, thought Lotti, dully. Poor, darling, naughty Federico. She had tried to rescue him and instead condemned him to death. She shivered, remembering her night in the coal cellar at school, the awful loneliness stretching on and on.

Lotti frowned. *The night that stretched on and on . . .*

Federico wasn't dead yet. There was a night, a whole night, in which to rescue him from the coal cellar. She could smuggle him down to the *Sparrowhawk!* Ben would help—Clara too, probably. Together they would find a way . . .

Lotti wriggled out of Sally's arms.

"Sally," she said. "Will you help me?"

How noisy a house is, when you need it to be quiet!

Lotti, fully dressed, lay under her bedcovers. She listened to her aunt and uncle come upstairs, heard the sound of the bathroom taps, their muffled voices, then at last silence. Shortly after midnight Sally tapped softly on Lotti's door and turned the key in the lock.

Down the landing they padded, as softly as possible, but how loud the squeak of the floorboards, how creaky the stairs . . . And Lotti's heart!

Surely, someone would hear her heart!

They paused in the hall to make sure no one was following, then crept toward the servants' corridor. As they approached the scullery, Federico heard them and began to howl.

"Soon as I open the door, you grab him and get him out of here," Sally hissed. "And for lawks' sake, make him shut up."

"What are *you* going to do?" whispered Lotti.

"I'm going to pile up the coal under the delivery hatch, then I'm going to shove it open. Make it look like the dog climbed up and pushed his way out."

"Uncle will never believe it."

"You got a better plan?"

Down into the coal cellar they went, and again Lotti shivered at memories of school. But then into her arms leaped Federico. She clamped her hand round his muzzle to silence him, at the same time showering him with kisses.

"Go," urged Sally.

In a world of shadows, under the beaming moon, Lotti and Federico ran through the garden and out on to the hills. They entered the woods. The scent of bluebells rose to meet them, heady and sweet in the night air. Lotti pushed away memories of her parents. Now was not the time to think of those lovely evenings lingering in the woods. But then as they approached the canal, a nightingale began to sing, and she doubled over with the punch of another memory.

Evening, high summer, overlooking a river, an adult voice singing in a garden.

Chante, rossignol, chante, toi qui a le cœur gai . . . Sing, nightingale, sing, you whose heart is light . . .

Lotti picked Federico up and held him close again.

No more running. Federico was saved, but they were still going to be separated. She was still being sent away.

Lotti, whose heart was not light but heavy, walked slowly the rest of the distance to the *Sparrowhawk*, to make her final moments with Federico last.

Chapter Nine

Ben couldn't sleep. After twisting and turning for hours in his berth, he pulled on his boots and sweater, gathered up his blanket, shook Elsie awake and went up with her onto the roof.

A strange day. First Lotti hadn't come to fetch him for lessons as she usually did. Secondly, when he went to Clara's alone, he found her door locked and a short note for him and Lotti pinned to its frame, explaining that she was going away. And thirdly . . .

Thirdly, this afternoon, another visit from Albert Skinner.

"Just wanted to let you know that I've written to the War Office," Albert had told Ben. "Asked to know when that brother of yours is coming home. Thought, coming from a policeman, maybe they'd give an actual date. I'm away until Wednesday to visit my own boy. Never quick, these things, but it's a few days since I wrote so hopefully there'll be an answer by the time I'm back."

That was all, but it had rocked Ben's world.

Soon, Albert would know the truth. And then what would happen? Up on the roof of the *Sparrowhawk*, Ben wrapped his arms round his body and hugged himself miserably.

How often he and Sam had slept up here in summer! Never well, but better than in the stuffy cabin. And in early August, Nathan always came up too, to watch the Perseids. They sat bundled together under blankets, drinking endless tea, making wish after wish as shooting stars fell from the sky. Ben loved the *Sparrowhawk* always, but never more than at night.

What would he wish for tonight, if he saw a star? That was easy. He would wish for Sam to come back. No, for Sam never to have gone. For Sam never to have gone, and Nathan to still be alive, and for the whole war never to have happened.

Oh, where was his brother?

Elsie had fallen asleep again, but now something roused her from her slumber, and she scrambled to her feet with a short bark of recognition. Ben followed her gaze and saw Lotti and Federico walking toward the *Sparrowhawk*.

He was surprised, of course, but also worried. It wasn't just that it was the middle of the night—there was something about the way Lotti was walking, slowly, as if she didn't want to arrive ... She stopped by the *Sparrowhawk* and looked up, and he saw that she had been crying. He held out a hand to help her up onto the roof, and Federico scrambled after her.

"What's happened?"

Lotti flung herself onto the blanket. "Oh, Ben, it's horrible!"

In chaotic order, she recounted the events of her day.

"Uncle Hubert was so angry," she concluded. "Maybe it *is* better if I go to school, even if they shut me in coal cellars and make me eat worms." She tried to smile, even as she raised her hand to rub her cheek where her uncle had hit her. Ben, who had been listening with growing anger, loved her for it. If he had an uncle who hit him and threatened to kill his dog, he didn't think he would be able to smile.

"I *will* be brave," Lotti continued, "but I need your help, Ben, to look after Federico. Will you? Because he will literally die if you don't."

"Lotti ..."

At the tone of Ben's voice, Lotti shuffled round. For the first time since she arrived it occurred to her that the hour was late, that the air was cold and that rather than wide awake and sitting on the roof, Ben should have been asleep in the cabin.

"Something's happened to you too."

Furiously, Ben blinked back tears. If Lotti could smile through her problems, the least he could do was not cry.

"Skinner," he grunted.

"*Constable* Skinner?"

"He's only gone and written to the War Office to ask when Sam's coming home."

Lotti gazed at him, as if expecting more. She didn't understand. How could she, when he had never told her the truth?

"But that's good, isn't it?" she asked. "Him being a policeman, maybe you'll get an answer at last. How long has it been since the last letter from the War Office?"

Ben glared at the canal, glinting in the moonlight.

"There was no letter from the War Office."

He had tried to sound calm, like lying for weeks to your best friend about something so fundamental was completely normal, but it came out sounding angry.

Lotti gasped. Ben stared harder at the canal.

"No letter?"

"No."

"You lied to me!" Lotti was outraged. "I didn't even know you *could* lie."

"It was the only way I could think not to go with

Mercy!" Ben defended himself. "I *had* to stay on the *Sparrowhawk*. What if Sam came back and I wasn't here? But now the War Office is going to tell Skinner Sam's *not* coming back, and then he's not going to let me carry on living here, is he? And then what'll happen to the *Sparrowhawk*? What'll happen to Elsie?"

His voice broke as he looked at his dog, fast asleep again on the blanket with her head in his lap. Lotti set aside her outrage.

"Tell me everything," she said. "Tell me *exactly*. Is Sam coming back or not? I'm confused."

Ben took a deep breath. Where should he start? "After Nathan was killed," he said slowly, "the man at the farmhouse where he was staying sent all his things back, with a letter explaining how the field hospital where Sam was being treated was destroyed. He . . . he said he buried Nathan himself, in the Protestant churchyard in the village. Mercy and I wrote back asking for news of Sam, but he didn't know—just that there were a lot of dead, and the wounded had been transferred to another hospital. Then later there was a telegram from the War Office . . ."

"You mean a letter," said Lotti.

"I keep telling you, there *was* no letter." It wasn't fair to be irritated with Lotti, but Ben couldn't help it. It wasn't her—it was the whole situation. "There was a telegram. It said Sam was *missing, believed killed.* And that's all."

"But then . . ."

"He *could* be alive," Ben insisted. "Believed killed doesn't mean *actually* killed. And I'd know, wouldn't I, if he was dead? I mean, I'd feel it. Didn't you, with your parents?"

Lotti had had not an inkling, not a hint of a tingle of a premonition that her parents had died until one of the servants told her, but she understood how important it was to Ben to believe that what he said was true. And so she didn't reply to his question but asked instead, "If Sam *were* alive, Ben, where would he be?"

"I don't know!" Ben's tears were back, and in danger of spilling over. "In France? The hospital was near a town called Buisseau, by a river. I remember the river because Nathan wrote that they brought the wounded there by barge. He joked that he should have taken the *Sparrowhawk* over to bring Sam home. Lotti, are you all right?"

Lotti had gone very still.

"Buisseau," she said. She felt dazed and a bit sick, because she could see clearly—so very, very clearly—the time she had driven through Buisseau with her parents, on their way to stay with Moune at Armande. They had stopped there for lunch. She remembered because it was the first time she had ever drunk pineapple juice, and to this day still felt the astonishment that something so delicious existed. But now wasn't the time to talk about pineapple juice and childhood holidays. Lotti, usually so easily caught up by emotion, knew instinctively that this memory went too deep, and that if she talked about the cool sweet juice and its attendant memories—a sunny café terrace in a dusty square, Mama's white dress, Papa's straw hat—they would sweep Ben and Sam and everything else away before them.

Ben didn't need memories, he needed practical solutions.

"Let's go and talk to Clara," said Lotti. "She'll know what to do."

"Clara's gone," said Ben, and pulled Clara's note from his pocket.

"*Gone to London, not sure when I'll be back,*" Lotti read. "Is that all?"

"That's all."

"Gone, right when we want her!"

"To be fair, she wouldn't have known that when she left."

They sat in silence, feeling betrayed and defeated, as a gentle breeze began to rise.

"We should run away," said Lotti.

"But where?" asked Ben.

The breeze grew stronger. The woods breathed out the scent of bluebells.

Where will we sail to, Lotti, on the ocean of blue?

And just like that, Lotti knew.

"France?"

Of all the outlandish things Lotti had ever said to Ben, this was the most outlandish yet.

"Yes! To find your brother! If he's alive ..."

"He *is* alive."

"But he hasn't written." Lotti raised an appeasing hand. "No, don't get angry, listen. *Why* hasn't he written?"

"I don't know," Ben muttered.

"Let's go inside," Lotti suggested. "I haven't eaten all day and I need food to be able to think."

In the cabin, Ben made tea while Lotti searched the food cupboard.

"Maybe Sam doesn't want to come back," she said as she searched. "But that seems unlikely, because why wouldn't he, when there's you and Elsie and the *Sparrowhawk*? More likely he's ill. Injured in the head, lying in some hospital just waiting for you to find him ..."

"*How?*" asked Ben. "*How* will we find him, when he's missing?"

With a cry of triumph, Lotti produced the biscuit tin and extracted a handful of Marie biscuits.

"We start with the site of the hospital that was bombed," she said with her mouth full. "We question the farmer Nathan stayed with. We visit the hospital where the wounded were taken. We ask every single person who works there if they've seen him. Do you have a photograph of him? Good. We show people the photograph. We don't leave until we find someone who remembers him."

"It'll never work," said Ben, but he felt his heart beat faster.

"How do you know if you don't try?" Lotti began to pace about the cabin. "Ben, aren't you tired of people telling you what to do? My whole life since my parents died, I've never got to decide. At school I couldn't even choose when to brush my teeth, or read a book, or just do nothing and daydream. And Barton's no better. Oh, I can get expelled and rescue Federico, but look at me now! Trying to hide him, about to be sent away again! And look at you! How long have you been waiting for Sam to come home? Months! And he's not here! Well, I don't *want* to let other people choose anymore. It's like what Clara taught us about. It's democracy. I want to be the one in charge! I say we go and we find Sam ourselves! And after that ..."

"After that, what?"

Lotti faltered. "Nothing."

She had been about to say, "maybe I could go and find my grandmother," but she wasn't sure how she felt about that. Moune's broken promise, the letters which suddenly stopped ... Lotti's fear of Moune's rejection was almost as great as her longing for her.

"Skinner's away," she continued. "I heard my uncle say. Do you know when he gets back?"

"Wednesday," said Ben. "But Lotti, how ..."

"Wednesday," Lotti interrupted. "And Clara's gone, doing whatever she's doing, and my uncle and aunt are off to Scotland in the morning ... I'm meant to go to school on Sunday ... it's perfect, Ben! We'll be miles away before anyone notices."

"Lotti! How will we *get* to France?"

She looked at him in astonishment. "Why, on the *Sparrowhawk*, of course!"

Ben felt a pinch of disappointment. He'd known all along the plan was impossible.

"We can't take the *Sparrowhawk* to France," he sighed.

"Why not? She's a boat, isn't she?"

"She has a completely flat bottom and no keel. Honestly, Lotti, you might as well try to get to France in a bathtub. She'd sink."

"But Nathan said he should have fetched Sam in her ..."

"It was a *joke*."

"It's worth a try!"

"Not if we *drown*."

"We'll be careful!"

"Careful, in the *Sparrowhawk*, on the sea?"

Lotti bit thoughtfully into a biscuit.

"What will happen to the *Sparrowhawk* if we *don't* go, Ben? What will happen to the dogs?"

"..."

"Will they let you keep Elsie if you go to an orphanage?"

"..."

"Because I don't think orphanages allow pets."

It was madness. It was dangerous. It was ... *irresistible*.

"We'll need provisions," Ben said. "Food, water, coal. I'll need to check the *Sparrowhawk* over properly. And we'll need a map. I've no idea how you get to France on a narrowboat, and I certainly don't know what to do when we get there."

Lotti grinned.

"We'll need money," Ben went on. "I don't have any, apart from my wages from the boatyard, and that won't get us far."

"I can get money." Lotti's eyes began to gleam.

Federico, sensing something was up, began to yap. Elsie woke and thumped her tail.

"And we'll have to go soon, to get as far away as possible before they all come back. Clara'll think it's strange we've gone, and Skinner's bound to come after us, and there'll be hell to pay when your uncle finds out you're not at school. I'll have to tell John Snell I can't work for him too—he'll worry if I don't turn up."

"We can leave tomorrow," said Lotti. "At night, so nobody sees us. Midnight! That's a good time to start an adventure. What else?"

"If we die, it'll be your fault."

Lotti burst out laughing and took another biscuit.

Chapter Ten

Lotti had been right: Uncle Hubert didn't believe for an instant that Federico had got out of the coal cellar alone. For a moment the next morning it looked like the whole Escape to France plan was doomed.

"Charlotte! CHARLOTTE! Where is the girl? Vera! The damn dog's escaped. Charlotte did this, I know she did. CHARLOTTE, COME DOWNSTAIRS THIS MINUTE!"

It was bad enough that Lotti should have disgraced the Netherburys in front of Lady Clarion. Now she had made her uncle look ridiculous in front of the lad come from Home Farm to shoot the dog. The lad had actually smirked on discovering Federico was gone, and remarked that he hadn't survived the war to shoot people's pets. Hubert Netherbury had taken it as a dig.

"CHARLOTTE!"

Sally appeared, clean as a pin in her uniform, not a trace of coal about her.

"Miss Lotti's still locked in her room from last night, sir. Shall I go and fetch her?"

"TELL HER I'M GOING TO WHIP HER!"

"That bolt on the coal cellar's been awfully loose lately, sir."

"SALLY, WERE YOU A PART OF THIS?"

"Hubert, dear." Rescue came in the unexpected form of Vera Netherbury walking down the stairs, dressed for traveling in a tweed suit, a silk scarf of Isobel's at her throat. "The taxi for the station is in the drive. Sally, please bring down the suitcases."

"TO HELL WITH SCOTLAND! I AM NOT GOING TO SCOTLAND UNTIL I'VE BEATEN THAT BRAT! AND SALLY, YOU'RE FIRED! FIRED, D'YOU HEAR ME?"

"Hubert, please don't speak to the staff like that. I know Charlotte has upset you dreadfully, but I for one am not going to let a naughty schoolgirl and a horrid little dog ruin my holiday. Sally, the suitcases."

The Netherburys and their luggage departed.

Lotti waited a few minutes to be sure they had gone, and crept downstairs to the study.

An oil painting hung behind Papa's desk, of Moune's

house overlooking the river at Armande. Lotti stopped for a moment to contemplate it. "Soon," she said.

Then, struggling a little because it was very big, she took the painting off the wall and revealed a safe.

Years ago, Papa had taught her the code of the combination lock, and Lotti hadn't forgotten it. "Just in case something happens to Mama and me," Papa had said. "It's where all the important stuff is kept."

Well, something had happened and now Lotti needed the stuff.

She held her breath as she turned the dial back and forth, until with a discreet click the lock was released and the door swung open.

The safe contained documents and Mama's jewels, all neatly stacked in pastel-colored cases. Lotti rifled through the documents for her passport, slipped it into her pinafore pocket, then began to look through the cases. The princess pearls Mama had worn to lunch parties . . . the garnets, which went with summer dresses, the emerald earrings Papa had given her one birthday and the sapphires Lotti had loved because they matched Mama's eyes. For a few minutes, Lotti was plunged into a world long lost, of parties and dinners, of spying on guests from the upstairs landing, of Mama sweeping into her room before dances to show off her frock, of perfumed kisses and the soft rustle of silk . . .

But she had a job to do.

From a slim puce case, she pulled a diamond necklace that Mama had never worn. "Because it is hideous!" Mama had once laughed. "It belonged to my great-aunt Agatha."

The necklace *was* hideous, but goodness how it glittered when Lotti held it up to the light! How much could it be worth?

"Lots, what are you doing?"

Sally stood in the doorway of the study, her hands on her hips and a suspicious expression on her face. Lotti shoved the diamonds behind her back, then reminded herself that Sally was her friend.

"Sal, where would you go if you wanted to sell a necklace?"

Sally came into the room and stared at the pile of gems on the floor. "Sell a necklace?"

How much should Lotti tell her?

"I have decided," she said carefully, "not to go school."

Sally whistled.

"I think," said Lotti, "it would be better for both of us if I didn't tell you where I'm going instead."

Sally grunted, then, reluctantly, nodded.

"So?" asked Lotti. "Where would you sell a necklace?"

"If you want quick money, you don't sell it, you take

it to a pawnbroker," said Sally. "But they won't deal with you, you're too young."

This was a blow, though hardly surprising. In a world controlled by adults, of course children weren't allowed to sell their own jewelry. That would be too easy. Lotti would have to be clever.

"Sally . . ."

"No."

"You don't know what I'm going to say!"

"I do. You're going to ask me to pawn that necklace for you, and I'm not doing it. I don't like your uncle and aunt, but I'm not stealing from them."

"You wouldn't be stealing from them!" explained Lotti. "Sally, it's *my* necklace! I inherited it. It is one hundred percent mine. And Sally . . . what if I said I'll give you some of the money from the necklace? As a wedding present. Toward your pub!"

Sally left, satisfied with the deal. Alone again, Lotti began to stack the jewelry cases back into the safe. Her eye fell on a new box, much smaller than the others, almost invisible at the back. Curious, she reached for it.

"Oh!"

Papa's signet ring, a family heirloom, a dark red carnelian engraved with the head of a falcon, in a gold setting carved with lilies. Papa had worn it sometimes for luck—though not, obviously, on the day of the crash.

"Well, we need luck now." Lotti took the ring out of its case and slipped it into her pocket. Then she finished putting the boxes back in the safe, locked it, and hoisted the painting back onto the wall, straightening it as best she could before hurrying out to prepare for the journey.

While Sally was in town, Lotti went round the pantry, shoveling items into a rucksack. Jam, margarine, biscuits. Tins of soup, peas, peaches, sausages, beans. From the store cupboard she took soap, tooth powder, matches, candles. She felt no more guilt at taking these than she had the necklace—they were bought with her money, after all. The only thing she felt bad about was lying when she said goodbye to Zachy.

"I'm going to school in the morning," she told him. "Thank you for everything you did for Federico. I didn't tell my uncle you helped me, by the way. He thinks I just hid him on the grounds."

Zachy winked, crinkling his walnut face. "You're a good 'un, Miss Lotti, just like your mama. I'm glad the little feller got away. And don't you fret about Barton while you're off at school. I'll take good care of the place for you till you're home, same as I always have."

Lotti hugged him and said, "You and Sally are the only things I'll miss."

Back at the house, Lotti went into the room where the jumble pile was stored, and rummaged through it for a pair of shorts, some boys' shirts, pajamas, trousers and a jersey. She took them back to her room and packed most of the clothes into her rucksack, along with her toothbrush, a comb and her share of the money Sally had brought back from Great Barton for the necklace.

There were only a few things left to do.

First, Lotti went into the bathroom. She stood before the mirror. In one hand, she held a lock of her long curly hair. In the other, a pair of sewing scissors. Snip, snip, snip . . . She cut her hair until it was as short as Ben's. Then she kicked off her boots, stepped out of her pinafore, peeled off her blouse and stockings, pulled on the shorts and jersey she had taken from the jumble and slipped her feet into a pair of rubber soled shoes. She looked at the mirror. A strange spiky haired creature looked back.

"Good," said Lotti, then she swept her cut hair into a pile and took it down to the kitchen to burn it.

Nobody was going to tell her how to dress again, or pull her by the hair.

In a final act of defiance, she marched into her aunt's bedroom and took back her mother's lovely shawl. Then she threaded her father's ring onto a piece of string and hung it round her neck.

By early evening, Lotti was ready, but she waited until it was dark before leaving, to reduce the chances of being seen. Shortly after nine o'clock, she shouldered her bulging knapsack, hugged Sally goodbye and set out across the garden of her childhood home.

At the gate, she stopped for a final look back.

"You and Sally are the only things I'll miss," she had told Zachy, but it wasn't true.

She would miss everything.

Ben was ready.

Working on the principle that the best lies are the ones closest to the truth, he had told John Snell that he was going to meet his brother, but kept vague about the details. John hadn't pressed him, offering instead, in lieu of final wages, to fill the *Sparrowhawk*'s fuel tank. Ben had driven her to the boatyard in the afternoon after his shift, and John had given him a map as a goodbye present. Back at the *Sparrowhawk*'s mooring, Ben had worked out the route they should take—along the canal network to join the Thames in London, then along the Thames Estuary all the way to the sea, round the Kent coast and out across the Channel to Calais. It was a lot more sea than Ben had anticipated, and he didn't like the look of the Thames either, which grew wider and wider as it snaked through London to the mouth of its estuary beyond. There would be tides to contend with, both on the sea and on the river ... and there would be currents, and other boats, big ones, cargo ships and military vessels, which could mow down the little *Sparrowhawk* and cut her in half without even noticing . . .

And then there were the people who might come after them—Clara, the Netherburys and Albert Skinner. Of these, the most immediate danger was from Albert Skinner. Ben did his calculations again: Albert wasn't due back in Barton until Wednesday. By then, the *Sparrowhawk* should have reached London, where the waterways were so busy she would just disappear.

Ben hoped . . .

It was an awful lot to think about—the physical danger, the risk of getting caught. But if they didn't go, Ben might lose everything—Elsie, the *Sparrowhawk*, all hope of finding Sam.

Pitched against this, Albert Skinner and the Thames and even the Channel were nothing.

Ben was *ready*.

Lotti arrived just after dark, bent almost double under her enormous rucksack. Federico greeted her ecstatically, and she laughed as she made a fuss over him, but when she looked up Ben saw that she had been crying again.

"What's happened?" he asked. "Is it your uncle?"

"No, no! He's gone, thank goodness. It's just . . . oh, I know Barton's not what it was, but I'm a little bit sad to leave, you know? Because I don't know when I'll see it again. You're so lucky, Ben, to be able to run away and take home with you."

Ben was dumbstruck. He had never thought of this before.

"Well," he said, a little diffidently because it felt like a very big thing to say, "the *Sparrowhawk*'s your home now too."

There was a brief, awkward pause in which they both felt suddenly overwhelmed by the enormity of what they were about to do.

"Your hair . . ." said Ben.

"Do you like it?" Lotti ran her hands over her shorn locks.

"It's terrible," Ben replied honestly. "And with the clothes as well . . . you look like a boy who's escaped from a workhouse."

"Good!" Lotti smiled faintly. "That means no one will recognize me. Maybe I'll call myself Charlie."

Another pause, then, "Where shall I put my things?"

"I made up Sam's berth for you," said Ben. Then, thinking how cramped the *Sparrowhawk* must seem compared to Barton Lacey, "I mean, unless you'd rather have the workshop . . ."

"No!" Lotti knew what Nathan's workshop meant to Ben. "It will be fun to share the cabin. And don't worry.

I will keep it absolutely shipshape! I'll be so tidy and quiet you won't even know I'm here!"

Ben snorted. "You! Tidy and quiet!" and just like that, the awkwardness was gone.

How many times had Lotti seen the *Sparrowhawk*'s cabin! Yet now that it was to be her home she drank in every little detail as if it were new, determined to love it with all her heart—the paintings of the birds and the little cat, the clever hooks and shelves, the curved candle sconces and the pot-bellied stove. She unpacked the food in the galley, then swung her rucksack onto Sam's berth and climbed after it to put away her things in the drawer at the foot of the mattress. When she had finished, she spread Mama's shawl over the covers.

"This is it," she told the little kingfisher by her pillow. "No more doing what other people say. This is where it starts."

They sat in the cabin to wait for midnight. When it was time, all four runaways went up to the rear deck. Ben took a deep breath to steady his nerves and asked Lotti to untie the moorings. Then, with the engine low, he steered the *Sparrowhawk* away from the bank.

A soldier sheltering for the night under the arches of the railway bridge gave a sleepy wave as she passed.

Other than him, nobody saw her go.

PART II

Chapter Eleven

Lotti learned to pilot the *Sparrowhawk* by the light of the moon on the deserted waters of the sleeping canal. It was Ben's idea, to relieve the tension which gripped them both in those first few hours, when neither of them could quite believe that some unforeseen enemy was not already on their tail. Lessons focused the mind.

They began to relax as dawn broke softly over the canal, preceded by a symphony of birdsong, and their surroundings came into view—a water meadow, grazing cows, a hawthorn hedgerow in flower, and not an enemy in sight. The canal grew busier. Slow and steady, Ben maneuvred the *Sparrowhawk* along, passing oncoming boats with inches to spare, responding to greetings with a nod as Nathan always used to. Beside him, seated on the storage seat, Elsie had assumed her habitual driving position: upright, ears flicked forward and muzzle raised as the breeze ruffled the hair around her neck. Ben felt a rush of love for her and for the *Sparrowhawk*. This was where he belonged, on the water with his dog and his boat. He could stay like this forever. He glanced over at Lotti, who was sitting opposite Elsie with Federico on her lap, her face tilted to the sun.

"All right?" he asked.

"More than all right," Lotti smiled.

About an hour after daybreak, when they had been going for over six hours, they stopped for a short rest. Ben brought the *Sparrowhawk* alongside the bank, and showed Lotti how to drive pegs into the ground to make a mooring. Then, while the dogs nosed about the towpath, Ben made tea while Lotti spread margarine and jam on slices of bread, and he explained the plan for the rest of the day.

"We'll get to our first lock at Emlyn this afternoon," he said. "I've been thinking. If I was a policeman and I was looking for a boat on the canals, the first thing I'd do is ask the lock-keepers if they'd seen her. Now, Skinner's not back till Wednesday, as we know. Hopefully, by the time he comes looking for the *Sparrowhawk*, no one will remember us. We just need to be as inconspicuous as possible."

"I've never even been in a lock before," said Lotti, a little nervously.

"You'll be fine," Ben assured her. "You just drive the *Sparrowhawk* and I'll do the rest."

They came to Emlyn Lock at about three o'clock and took their place at the back of a queue of boats waiting to go through.

"It's good that there are lots of other boats," said Ben. "Means it's less likely anyone will remember us. And I can't actually see the lock-keeper, only that girl over there with the baby."

Lotti looked in the direction Ben was indicating and saw a girl of about fourteen standing by the lock with a baby on her hip, talking to the helmsman of a narrowboat which had just pulled in.

"I don't see why that helps," she said. "Skinner could interview her just as well as a lock-keeper."

"Yes, but nobody's ever interested in what children say."

Two boats had gone into the lock, one behind the other. Ben edged the *Sparrowhawk* forward, then stopped again, tucked into the bank. There was just one boat ahead of them now.

"We'll be going in after the *Marianne*," said Ben. "I'll

get off before you drive in to work the lock. All you need to do is follow the *Marianne*, slow and steady and turn off the engine. Right, here we go, the lock's opening again. Ready?"

"Ready!" said Lotti, with airy confidence.

With a thrill of nervous excitement, she took hold of the tiller. Federico leaped up onto the storage box beside her. Lotti grinned and pulled one of his ears.

"Bet you never dreamed we'd be doing *this* when I rescued you!"

A pair of ducks flew overhead and landed in the water behind the *Sparrowhawk*. Federico turned to look at them, whiskers quivering.

"Don't get any thoughts in your head," Lotti warned. "We don't want a repeat of the pheasant. Not here. Here we have to be absolutely, completely invisible."

The lock gates opened. Two boats came out. The first didn't stop, but the second pulled in just behind the *Sparrowhawk*, close enough for Lotti to see the details of the painted bird perched on the curling letters of her name, the *Secret Starling*.

How strange, thought Lotti. I feel as if I've seen that boat before.

But the *Marianne* was already entering the empty lock. Ben stepped off the *Sparrowhawk* and called down to Lotti to move on. Eyes narrowed in concentration, she pushed the speed lever forward and began to steer . . .

"Watch out for Federico," Ben called. "Elsie's used to locks, but it might scare him."

But Federico wasn't scared at all. Federico was watching the ducks, still paddling in the water . . .

His whiskers twitched.

Slow and steady, the *Sparrowhawk* followed the *Marianne* into the lock. Ben began to close the gates behind her. Lotti, careful to be invisible, tried to look as if she had done this many times before, but inwardly she was cheering.

Her first lock!

The downhill gates closed behind the *Sparrowhawk*. The sluices on the uphill gates, ahead of the *Marianne*, began to let in water.

The *Sparrowhawk* and the *Marianne* began to rise.

Federico scrambled off the storage box onto the roof of the *Sparrowhawk*, took a short run and leaped, aiming for the edge of the lock.

Chapter Twelve

What happened next was spectacular, no doubt about it. Everyone who was there agreed—the girl with the baby, the crew of the *Marianne* in the lock with the *Sparrowhawk*, the crews of the *Lily Rose* and the *Princess* waiting to come through, the crew of the *Secret Starling*.

Federico, having leaped, missed his landing. For a split second, he clawed onto the edge of the lock with his front paws, scrabbling frantically with his back legs against the wall. It seemed as if he would slide back into the water and either be crushed between the wall and the *Sparrowhawk*, or drowned, or both. Then, with an impressive display of agility, he heaved himself up and over the edge of the lock. For a moment he stood still, getting his bearings. From the tiller of the *Sparrowhawk*, Lotti yelled at him to stay. Ignoring her, he raced away, past the *Marianne*, past the lock and flung himself into the canal at the ducks.

The ducks took off, as ducks always do.

And Federico ... Federico tried to swim, but the water was being sucked toward the lock, dragging him under. Federico fought, managed to surface, was pulled under again, and once more fought his way back up. He was pulled a third time, and now he was tired ...

On the bank, people were shouting. Federico caught a glimpse of the girl with the baby, the man from the *Marianne* ... And Lotti! His Lotti, screaming at him from the *Sparrowhawk*, and Ben running toward him ...

There was a splash, too heavy for Lotti. A splash and a deep voice swearing at him, using words Federico had only ever heard before from Malachy Campbell, and there was a sort of metal pole and a net and, as the crews of half a dozen narrowboats cheered, he was lifted out of the canal like a fish, and deposited shivering and dripping on the bank.

The lock gates opened, the *Marianne* and the *Sparrowhawk* came out. The *Marianne* went on her way, her crew waving. A shaking Lotti pulled the *Sparrowhawk* alongside the bank a safe distance from the lock and waited for Ben to help her moor up.

"So much for being inconspicuous," he hissed as he arrived.

"It's not my fault!" she protested.

"I told you to watch out for him!" said Ben, but Lotti was already running back to the towpath where Federico, with a shocking lack of gratitude, was shaking water all over his rescuer. With a cry, Lotti scooped the little dog into her arms.

The man who had rescued Federico was called Frank. He was the skipper of the *Secret Starling*, about forty years old, completely bald under his flat cap and dressed in an ancient patched jacket. He was also wet to his waist, and very cross.

"Lucky for you I keep a fishing net on the *Starling*," he snarled at Lotti. "Lucky me and my brother Jim skipped our lunch earlier and stopped for a bite before moving on. Lucky Jim heard you scream, and is softer'n me and said we should help."

"Lucky Frank's not as tough as he makes out and said yes." Jim, who had walked over from the *Secret Starling* along with the girl and the baby, was as cheerful as Frank was grumpy, with thick brown hair and a spray of forget-me-nots in the buttonhole of his corduroy jacket. "Lucky he didn't think twice about it."

Lotti, still holding Federico, held out a hand to Frank.

"My name is Charlie," she told him. "And I'm forever in your debt. I'm sorry you got wet, and I'm *very* sorry about my dog. When it comes to birds he is appallingly behaved. I don't know that I can ever thank you enough."

"All right, all right," grumbled Frank, and they all pretended not to notice that he had gone a deep beetroot red. "No need to go on about it."

The brothers returned to the *Secret Starling* and drove away, Lotti enthusiastically waving them off.

"Well!" said the girl with the baby. "That was exciting."

Her name was Molly and she was the lock-keeper's daughter. Her parents had left her in charge of the lock and the baby while they went to London to fetch Molly's sister, Martha, who was just back from the war, driving ambulances in Central Europe.

"I wanted to go too," said Molly.

"To London?" asked Lotti.

"To Central Europe," said Molly. "But they wouldn't let me. Said I'm too young."

"Grown-ups are horribly unfair," Lotti said sympathetically. "Believe me, we know."

Molly's eyes flicked over the *Sparrowhawk*. "Where are *your* parents?"

"Dead," said Lotti. "We're running away. Will you help us?"

≈ ≈ ≈

"I don't understand!" fumed Ben, when Emlyn Lock was safely behind them. "Why did you tell her we were running away?"

He was angry and Lotti was sorry for it, but she felt very calm.

"Molly liked us," she said. "She thought we were exciting and she's *longing* for excitement. She wanted to go to Central Europe! And I think, Ben, though I'm very good at lying, sometimes it's better to tell the truth. I didn't tell her much; I didn't give any details. All I asked was that if a policeman comes, she tells him she hasn't seen us."

"A lot of use that will be. About a million other people saw us. They were *cheering* us!"

"I know," said Lotti. "But Molly is the one Constable Skinner is most likely to ask. Don't be cross, Ben. It will be all right, I promise. Let's stop soon and eat and take the dogs for a walk before they get up to any more mischief. We've been miles and miles already, and Constable Skinner doesn't even know the *Sparrowhawk*'s gone yet."

"I'm not stopping," said Ben. "Not until we get to France."

But soon he began to yawn, and once he had started

the yawns just kept on coming. Lotti was right. There was no reason to push themselves further today, especially after such an early start.

A couple of miles after leaving Emlyn Lock, they came to a lovely stretch of canal, wide and quiet, with woodland on one side and meadows on the other, where they moored for the night. They gathered wood to make a fire, and with these comforting, familiar actions Ben's anger began to dissipate.

When the flames had died sufficiently, he brought a grill from the *Sparrowhawk* and put it over the embers to cook sausages.

"I've been thinking about Clara," he said as he cooked. "Do you think we should have left her a note explaining what we are doing?"

Lotti, who still hadn't forgiven Clara her own short little note, said, "She'd only come after us and try to stop us."

The sausages, salty and slightly charred, cooked in the open air and shared with the dogs, were delicious. After they had eaten, Ben and Lotti took the dogs for a walk along the towpath until they came to a tunnel. Lotti leaned over the water to peer in, cupped one hand over her mouth and hooted. A faint echo hooted back.

"We should camp in here," she said. "No one would ever find us."

"Apart from all the other boats coming through." Ben yawned again. "And you're not allowed to stop in tunnels. It's a law. Come on, I have to sleep."

When they came back to the *Sparrowhawk*, bats were swooping over the meadow. The dogs flopped instantly asleep, but despite their tiredness Lotti and Ben stayed up on deck a little longer, unwilling to let the day go. Night fell and a barn owl sailed past like a ghost.

"A good omen," Ben said.

Stars punctured the sky and the world felt perfect.

Ben and Lotti went to bed, intending to rise before dawn again the following day to continue their journey. But the peace of the evening, the beauty of the night, were too powerful. It was their first night sleeping alone on the *Sparrowhawk* and it felt delicious.

They slept late into the next morning.

How could they have known that Albert Skinner was already on their trail?

An outbreak of whooping cough at his son's nursing home having cut short Albert's visit, he had returned to Great Barton late on Sunday afternoon. On his way home he stopped at the police station, where he found a letter from the War Office, informing him that there had been no news of Sam Langton since he was reported missing, believed killed ten months ago.

With a heavy heart, Albert went to the *Sparrowhawk* to tell Ben. On seeing that she was missing from her usual mooring, he went to Clara Primrose's cottage. On finding her absent, he went to the boatyard to speak to John Snell.

"Gone to find his brother," John said. "Didn't say where."

"But his brother's dead. Well, missing, but it's the same thing."

"Just telling you what he told me."

Gone to find his brother. It made no sense.

Albert was weary, and Albert was sad. He had been looking forward to a few days visiting his boy, who was beginning to show signs of recovering from his own war injury. But Albert was also conscientious. As Ben had predicted, he set out to interview the lock-keepers.

The first uphill lock was only a mile out of town. Albert walked over to it after speaking to John Snell, but the keeper there had not seen the *Sparrowhawk*. It was too late to go downhill all the way to Emlyn today. He decided to borrow a police car in the morning, and drive out to it first thing.

Far away in London, Clara lay in bed in her friend Kitty's spare room, hugging her pillow close as if it could somehow take away her grief.

Max was dead. Not *missing, believed* but *proper, no doubt about it* dead. She had received a letter from a lawyer informing her of this, and inviting her to his office for a meeting.

"He made a will," the lawyer told her, as if this somehow made things better. "He left everything to you. His family are very unhappy about it, that's why it's taken so long to inform you. You understand."

No, Clara wanted to say, she didn't understand. Her own parents had thrown her out of their home because of Max. His mother did not answer her letters. Clara didn't see why she should be understanding at all, but she didn't want to seem rude.

"I can't imagine he had anything much to leave," she said instead. "He wasn't rich."

"Ah," said the lawyer.

And he told her that Max's collection of love and war poems, the one which was named after her, had become a bestseller, and that all the royalties were to go to her.

"I mean, it's not *millions*," the lawyer said, as he handed her a check. "Poetry is poetry, after all. But it is *something*."

Clara had cried for two days, and now there were no tears left, only an awful emptiness and the question: what was she going to do with her life, now that the waiting was over?

Chapter Thirteen

A thunderous rapping on the cabin door jerked Lotti and Ben out of sleep. They both jumped, then froze.

"Is it Skinner?" whispered Lotti, hanging upside down from the top berth.

"It can't be," said Ben. "He's still away."

"Then who . . ."

"How should I know any better than you?"

"Pretend we're not in."

But the dogs were already howling. Ben reached for his shorts and sweater.

"Take a frying pan," Lotti advised, as he climbed down from his berth. "As a weapon, in case it's a murderer."

Ignoring Lotti, Ben unlocked the cabin hatch, blinking in the sunlight as the dogs streamed out past him. Lotti dashed to the galley for the frying pan, pulling on her clothes as she went, then ran up to the deck after Ben, prepared for battle. When she saw who their visitors were, she put down the pan and laughed with relief.

"Molly! And baby Philip!"

The lock-keeper's daughter stood on the deck with her baby brother strapped to her chest in a shawl. A bicycle lay on the bank behind her. She was panting.

"Just let me catch my breath," Molly gasped. "All right, listen. There's a copper come to the lock this morning all the way from Great Barton, looking for Ben." She glanced at Lotti. "He didn't say nothing about Charlie."

"Skinner?" Ben looked appalled. "But he's supposed to be away!"

"I don't know his name," Molly said. "Little feller, sort of pigeon feet."

"Skinner," sighed Lotti.

"He's at our house now. I asked Martha to make him tea to slow him down—I didn't say why, don't worry. But this copper, right, he's not giving up. I did what you asked, said I'd been out by the lock all of yesterday and I'd remember a boy alone on a boat, especially one that looks like this, but that I didn't see you." Her eyes rounded as she considered what she had done. "I lied to a copper!"

"What do you mean, he's not giving up?" demanded Lotti.

"Soon as he's finished his tea, he says he's going to the next lock at Anfield. In case I missed you, he says. And then *Mum* only went and offered to lend him a bicycle so he can follow the canal!" Molly paused briefly to mark her disgust with her parent, before concluding, "So I came to warn you, because it's not far and if you get going fast, maybe you can get through before he arrives."

"You see, Ben?" said Lotti. "I *told* you we could trust Molly!"

She jumped onto the towpath and began to undo the mooring lines, calling for the dogs.

"Ben, what are you waiting for?" she shouted, as the dogs jumped back on board. "Let's go!"

"Go where?" Ben felt very tired. They were defeated and he knew it. "We can't outrun a bicycle, even with Skinner riding it. And even if we did—do you think the keeper at Anfield will be as nice as Molly, and lie about us?"

Lotti slumped. An image of her uncle loomed over her. There must be something they could do, there must be . . .

"The tunnel!" she cried. "If we can make it to the tunnel, we can hide in there!"

"We can't hide in a tunnel," said Ben. "It's not allowed."

Lotti turned on him in disbelief. "Ben, *none* of this is allowed!"

Barefoot on the towpath, she began to pace. "We hide in the tunnel, Constable Skinner goes to the second lock, the lock-keeper says he hasn't seen us, Constable Skinner leaves. Molly, will you be a hero and let us know when the coast is clear?"

Blushing with pleasure at being included, Molly said, "I will."

Ben's mind raced. "We're too slow. We'll never make it."

"We have to try, Ben! Molly, is there any way you can slow him down?"

"Yes!" A fierce expression crossed the lock-keeper's daughter's face, and she began to undo the shawl which contained her baby brother.

"Take Philip!" she ordered, thrusting him at Lotti.

"What? No! Molly! Molly, come back!"

"No time to explain!" shouted Molly, as she cycled off. "Take him. I'll get him back later! Go!"

There was no time for thinking, only action.

Lotti shut the dogs in the cabin—nobody wanted a repeat of the duck episode right now—then stood by Ben's side as he drove away from their mooring, clutching an indignant baby Philip.

"Can't you go faster?" she begged.

If you have ever been on a narrowboat, you will know that they are not boats you can rush. Narrowboats are not like sailing yachts. They are heavy and take a long time to respond. Slow and steady, that is how narrowboats work best, with small commands. Otherwise disaster ensues.

Against his better judgment, Ben pushed the speed lever forward. Philip, alarmed by the sudden noise, bellowed and kicked out, his foot catching Ben's elbow. Ben jolted the tiller. He tried to correct the movement, but it was too late.

The *Sparrowhawk* tilted toward the edge of the canal, hit the bank and stopped.

Ben swore, loudly and extensively.

"What happened?" cried Lotti.

"We're stuck," said Ben. "The canal edges must be silted up. Just hope the propeller doesn't get caught, or we'll never get out ..."

On the roof of the *Sparrowhawk* there was a strong pole for exactly this sort of situation. As calmly as he could, Ben told Lotti to put the baby down and use the pole to push off the bank. Lotti, also trying to be calm, went into the cabin, laid Philip on Ben's berth, and wedged him in with pillows.

"Stay here," she ordered the dogs, who regarded the baby with amazement. "Look after him."

Then she ran back onto the deck, jumped onto the roof, seized the pole and drove it into the bank.

"Push!" shouted Ben. "Push as hard as you can!"

Slowly, slowly, the *Sparrowhawk* floated away from the bank and they continued toward the tunnel.

Slowly, slowly, with a policeman on their tail . . .

Molly sighted Albert Skinner about a mile short of the tunnel.

"Right, my girl," she told herself firmly. "You can do this."

It was going to hurt, but she knew she *had* to do it. For Ben and Lotti and the mad, sweet dog who nearly drowned, but also for children everywhere who should be free to have adventures without their parents. And for her own sake too, she realized with a chill, because what on earth would her mum say if the copper caught up with the *Sparrowhawk* and found baby Philip on board?

What on earth would her mum *do*?

Molly clenched her teeth, tightened her hold on the handlebars and pedalled as hard as she could toward the oncoming policeman.

WHOOSH! CLANG! CRASH!

For about a second and a half, as Molly sailed through the air over her bicycle, Albert Skinner's bicycle and Albert Skinner himself, it was almost fun.

Then—well, yes. It did hurt.

Molly's tears didn't stop Albert Skinner's pursuit, but they improved the fugitives' lead. By the time he had regained his own composure, calmed Molly and checked both himself and his bicycle for damage, the tunnel had swallowed the *Sparrowhawk* completely.

Albert Skinner, as the plotters had hoped, cycled on toward Anfield Lock.

Chapter Fourteen

The *Sparrowhawk* hunkered in the gloom. Ben had cut the engine and he and Lotti lay on their backs on the cabin roof with their feet braced against the tunnel ceiling, to stop the *Sparrowhawk* from drifting. At either end of the tunnel, they could just make out half moons of daylight, but in the middle where they were, the darkness was almost absolute. Their hearts were beating fast, and their breathing came out loud and ragged.

"What if another boat comes?" whispered Ben.

"It can pass us," said Lotti, but she wasn't sure this was true. It was hard to tell in the dark, but the canal looked awfully narrow.

"What if it passes Skinner after it's seen us?" hissed Ben. "What if he asks the crew if they've seen the *Sparrowhawk*?"

"We just have to hope that won't happen," whispered Lotti.

Then they were quiet and in the quiet and the dark, thoughts came: of what would happen after Albert Skinner found them, of Hubert Netherbury's anger and the loss of the *Sparrowhawk* and the dogs . . .

"Is the baby all right?" whispered Ben, to chase away his fears.

"He's fine. The dogs are looking after him."

But Lotti was wrong. Baby Philip was not fine. From the moment his sister shoved him into Lotti's arms, his indignation had been growing. Until now, there had been just enough distractions to stop that indignation from tipping into full-blown rage, but now he was alone, and it was dark, and in the dark the dogs were snuffling and he was afraid.

Baby Philip began to whimper. The dogs, who were still baffled by him but had accepted him as one of their own, yipped and whined in sympathy. Baby Philip wailed. The dogs yowled. Their combined cries bounced off the walls of the tunnel like the howls of souls in torment. The children cursed under their breath. Lotti swung off the roof and climbed down to calm them all. As she reached the cabin steps her heart skipped a beat. The half moon of bright daylight at the entrance of the tunnel behind the *Sparrowhawk* had disappeared, replaced by the soft glow of a boat's navigation light . . .

Another boat had entered the tunnel behind them.

Up on the roof, Ben froze. What should he do? He knew that the *Sparrowhawk* had no right to stop in the tunnel, but he couldn't move on now! How long did Albert Skinner need to get to the lock at Anfield? And to come back again? If they could only have a few more minutes . . .

The *Sparrowhawk* swayed as the other boat drew near. Ben blinked in its approaching light but didn't move from his position on his back with his feet braced against the tunnel ceiling. The other boat's engine died down. From below, Ben heard Lotti desperately try to shush the howling baby and the dogs, then . . .

"Well, blow me down," said a familiar voice as the other boat came alongside the *Sparrowhawk*. "If it ain't our old friends!"

It was a sort of miracle, really. Not only that the other boat should be the *Secret Starling*, but also that Jim should be so good with babies.

There was no conversation possible while Philip was crying. The *Starling* pulled up beside the *Sparrowhawk*, Jim threw her center line up to Ben, hopped aboard and took the sobbing Philip in his arms. With a few practiced bounces and a firm rub of his back, he brought the wailing back to whimpering. With the heel of a loaf fetched by Lotti from the galley, the whimpering turned to slurps. And with a click of Jim's fingers, the dogs sat, then lay, in a silent heap at his feet.

"Raised a baby myself," Jim explained, as Lotti looked on with amazed gratitude. "My brother Jack. Comes in useful. You're gonna have to change him soon, though."

"I think we'll just give him back," said Lotti. "I really don't want another one."

"Change his nappy, I mean," grinned Jim. "Not swap the little darling. Where d'you get him anyway? You didn't have him yesterday."

"Case anyone hadn't noticed, we're stopped in the middle of a blinking tunnel!" Frank's voice floated down toward them from the *Starling*. "Jim, stop nattering and find out what the blinking problem is."

But Jim wasn't listening. One hand on baby Philip's belly, he was staring at the birds painted around the cabin.

"Well, would you look at that . . . I knew I remembered the *Sparrowhawk*. Here, hold the nipper."

Jim jumped off the *Sparrowhawk* and back onto the *Starling* and down into her cabin. He came back out again holding a small painted piece of wood, then, ignoring a bellow of rage from his brother, jumped back onto the *Sparrowhawk*.

Ben lowered his legs and peered down from the roof.

"What's going on?" he asked.

Before Lotti could answer, Jim let out a shout.

"I was right!"

"What ..."

"All them birds!" Jim handed Lotti the piece of wood he had taken from his cabin. Painted on it was the delicate figure of a starling, and beneath the starling, just like beneath the robin over Ben's berth, and the kingfisher above Sam's, and every bird Nathan had ever painted, the tiny letters NL. Lotti took a deep breath. She knew now why the *Secret Starling* had seemed familiar to her when she came out of Emlyn Lock. She took the little piece of wood in her hands and handed it up to Ben.

"Ben, look!"

He took the little painting from her hands. She saw his eyes widen with shock, then cloud with something else that she recognized—the heavy dullness of a long and lingering grief.

"The *Sparrowhawk*!" Jim exclaimed. "Nathan Langton! It's all coming back now—he painted the sign on the *Starlin'* for us, then gave us this one as a present for our little brother, Jack, who was down in the dumps because he 'ad a cold. Well, I never! Your dad, is he? I didn't even know he was married, let alone had kids."

Lotti, still holding the baby, wished that Jim would stop talking. The way Ben gently stroked the little starling, as if it weren't a painting at all but something alive and tender, made her want to cry.

With characteristic bluntness, Frank brought everyone back to their current situation.

"Touching though this is, I don't like breaking the law unless I 'ave to," he said. "And right now, I don't see why I 'ave to, so let's get a move on, shall we, and take this outside."

Oh, thought Lotti agonizingly, where was Molly? Why was she taking so long?

"The thing is," she started, then stopped, wondering how to explain without giving too much away that the *Starling* should go but the *Sparrowhawk* would linger a little longer in the tunnel.

"You in trouble?"

Lotti was to grow to love Frank very much, but in that moment he was terrifying. Even in the darkness, she saw his eyes glint.

"There's a policeman after us," she admitted.

"A policeman?" Frank growled.

"We haven't done anything wrong!" said Lotti. "Not really."

"Where is he?" demanded Frank.

"Somewhere between here and Anfield Lock. Our friend's going to tell us when the coast is clear."

"Frank," said Jim. "They're Nathan's kids."

Something passed between the two brothers, a secret understanding.

"Right," grunted Frank. "Charlie, you can explain later. For now, stay here. Jim, take the nipper, keep him quiet. You two, don't make a noise. We'll go ahead. If the copper sees us coming out, he'll assume there's no one in the tunnel."

"And if he asks, we'll tell him we ain't seen no one," said Jim. "That'll send him on his way."

The *Secret Starling* was gone within seconds. Ben and Lotti resumed their position on the roof.

"Are you all right?" Lotti whispered.

"Yes," he said. "It was just a shock, you know? Hearing them talk about Nathan like that. And seeing that little starling he painted for them. It was like ..."

"Like having a bit of Nathan back." Lotti's hand went to Papa's ring, on its string around her neck. "I know."

"Wasn't it lucky though, to run into the *Starling?*" she whispered. "Imagine if it had been another boat! We'd have had to move, wouldn't we?"

Ben cursed. "Oh no . . ."

"What is it?"

"There *is* another boat."

Lotti turned to look, and sure enough, there it was, blocking the light to the tunnel, its navigation light growing brighter and its engine louder as it came toward them. She turned back to Ben, eyes wide with fear.

"Ahoy ahead!" called a man's voice. "Everything all right there?"

"Propeller jammed, but it's all right now!" Ben called back. Then, shakily, to Lotti, "What do we do?"

"I don't know!"

"Move it, will you?" the voice shouted. "I've got a cargo of blinking chickens and they're doing my head in."

In a daze, Ben rolled off the roof and fired the engine.

"Go slowly," urged Lotti. "Go very, very slowly."

With their hearts in their mouths, they chugged toward the tunnel exit. Lotti squeezed her eyes shut. She would not think about her uncle, she would not, or the lad from Home Farm and his gun. She would think of nice things, of snuggling with Federico, of the garden at Armande . . .

The air warmed up, she could feel light on her eyelids . . .

"Can you see Skinner?" she breathed.

Ben began to laugh.

"Open your eyes, Lotti. You've never seen anything like it."

Lotti opened her eyes. On the canal bank, a little bent, lay Molly's bicycle, with Frank beside it almost smiling. And on the roof of the *Secret Starling*, waving and cheering, stood Jim and Molly, with a clean and splendidly naked baby Philip in her arms.

There was no sign of Albert Skinner.

Chapter Fifteen

The *Sparrowhawk* was moored behind the *Secret Starling*. Both crews, Molly, the baby and the dogs sat on the bank beside her, drinking tea. Molly—with grazed elbows and knees, and impressive bruises coming up on her shins—had given a breathless account of her encounter with Albert Skinner. Jim had told the story of how Albert called out to the *Starling* as she emerged from the tunnel, asking if they'd seen a narrowboat called the *Sparrowhawk* crewed by a lad on his own with a black and white dog, and how he, Jim, had pretended to think about it and then said no, he hadn't. Lotti had thanked everyone rapturously, and Ben had thanked them more quietly, and the dogs had caught the general excitement and capered madly about. But now the dogs were asleep, and the baby too, and a not very comfortable silence had fallen because Frank, eyes glinting again as they had in the tunnel, had just said to Lotti, "Right, Charlie. Explain."

Lotti looked at Ben, trying to ask just with her eyes how much she should say. Ben shrugged back that he didn't know.

"I'm not sure where to start," Lotti hedged.

Frank gave her a hard stare.

"Start with your dad," said Jim. "Nathan. How come he's not here?"

Lotti swallowed and began.

"Nathan's not my dad," she said. "He was Ben's, but then he died."

She told them everything. She spoke of a lovely house and a big garden, of a charmed life and an airplane crash, of unkind relatives and the loneliness of boarding school. She spoke of beatings and sewing mistresses, of caged dogs and diamonds, of the farm hand sent to kill Federico and of Clara Primrose's wonderful lessons, of cutting off her hair so nobody would ever pull it again.

As Lotti spoke, Molly's and Jim's eyes grew rounder. Frank's frown, deeper.

Ben took over and, more diffidently, spoke of orphanages and the kindness of strangers, of a childhood spent on the water and the coming of war, of a brother wounded and a father gone to comfort him, of bombs falling on hospitals and letters to the War Office, of believed killed not being *actually* killed, of their plan to go to France.

"France . . ." sighed Molly, and her imagination soared.

"France!" grinned Jim, and anything was possible.

"France," growled Frank, and reality landed with a thump.

"We know it won't be easy," Lotti acknowledged. "With the copper, and the Channel and the *Sparrowhawk* built for canals, but . . ."

"I'll say it won't be easy," sniffed Frank. "You won't even make it past Anfield Lock. What do you think that lock-keeper's going to do when he sees you, now that copper's been asking questions?"

"Call the copper," admitted Lotti, her heart sinking.

"Gotta love 'em though, Frank," said Jim gently. "Going all the way to France to find the lad's brother."

"On a blinking narrowboat!" said Frank. "I know the Channel, and I'm telling you it's not meant for a narrowboat. Boats like ours are made for flat water."

"What'll happen to the *Sparrowhawk* on the sea?" whispered Molly.

"She'll sink!" snapped Frank. "You'd better pray for good weather. With a calm sea, you might stand a chance, if you don't get lost. Slightest hint of a swell and she'll be gone under the first wave."

Molly swallowed and hugged baby Philip close.

"I reckon we should help them though, Frank," murmured Jim.

"Help them kill themselves? I've a mind to run after that copper right now."

"Come on, Frank! You've seen how the lad handles the boat. I reckon he could have a fair go."

Frank snorted. "Say they do make it across, then what? Two kids alone in a country that's been blinking torn apart by war . . ."

"That starling . . ." Jim continued softly. "Remember our Jack, before he went away? Spent ages copying it on a scrap of paper till it was just right, and kept it in his pocket. Said he didn't know if they had starlings where he was going, but whenever he looked at it he'd think of home. Said it would bring him luck."

Something passed over Frank's closed face, a grimace of loss and love.

Lotti knew that look. It was the one we keep for those no longer with us. And she knew without asking that Frank and Jim's little brother had gone away to the war, and that he had not returned.

Jim said, "Let's help them through the next few locks at least."

With a weary sigh, Frank nodded.

They said goodbye to Molly and Philip, and then the *Starling* and the *Sparrowhawk* went on their way, with the *Starling* leading. At Anfield Lock, the keeper narrowed his eyes at the *Sparrowhawk*. Frank asked, almost lazily, "All right, Pete?" before stepping—no, *strolling*—ashore.

"What you lot waiting for?" he yelled over his shoulder. "Lock's not gonna fill itself! Jump to it—Jim, you do the gates. The kids'll drive."

"What's he doing?" Lotti whispered to Jim as Frank and the lockkeeper stepped aside, deep in conversation.

"Sorting it." Jim winked. "Don't you worry, Charlie. Frank can sort anything. You just drive. It'll be all right, you'll see."

"What did you tell him?" Ben called across the water, once they had come through the lock.

Just for a second, Frank's granite features softened.

"Popular man, your dad," he said. "Pete won't say nothing. And he'll spread the word. Nobody'll say nothing. Nobody'll rat on Nathan's kid."

Word got out among the lock-keepers. After a few locks, it was no longer necessary for Frank to mention Nathan at all. Nonetheless, as the *Starling* was also going to London, Frank suggested that the two boats continue to travel together. As Jim put it, "Two kids on their own, people ask questions. If there's adults about, they leave 'em alone."

Molly longed for adventure, but Frank had frightened her. What if the *Sparrowhawk* did sink, immediately, straight to the bottom of the sea? For two days she worried over Lotti and Ben's secret, wondering if she should do something to stop them. By Wednesday morning, knowing the *Sparrowhawk* would be coming into London and that soon it would be too late, she confessed everything to her sister, Martha.

Martha, who had grown very practical since driving ambulances around Central Europe, went straight to Great Barton to speak with Clara Primrose.

"I didn't want to go to the police," Martha said to Clara, "on account of our Molly mowing down that copper on a bicycle. I don't want to get her into trouble. But in the whole story, you sounded like the only one who cared for them kids."

Clara had returned to Great Barton on Monday, intending to get on with her life, only to find that her life had moved on without her. Ben and the *Sparrowhawk* were gone; Hubert Netherbury had written informing her that she was fired and that Lotti was going away. She had been upset they hadn't left a note, but as she listened to Martha's story she began to understand why.

"They thought I'd stop them," she said.

"Well, you would, wouldn't you?" said Martha.

"I can't really believe it," said Clara. "It's such an incredible story. But rather beautiful too."

"It's barmy, that's what it is."

After Martha had gone, Clara sat thinking about what she should do. Of course Martha was right. It *was* a barmy story. Sailing the *Sparrowhawk* across the Channel! Looking for Sam! How exactly did they propose to find him? Clara knew what had happened to Sam—the same thing that had happened to millions of other souls who had gone missing, shot to pieces on a battlefield. That's what *missing* meant. It was brutal, but true. She wished Ben had spoken to her before setting off, and that Lotti had come to her about poor little Federico. To be sure, Clara had been away, but they might have waited and she would have helped.

Well, they were gone now. The question was, what should Clara do?

Catch up with them! she thought, jumping up from her chair to walk about the room. Stop them before they killed themselves on the sea, get Lotti back to school before the Netherburys returned on Friday, make Ben see sense about his brother. He and Elsie could live with her—why not? She had money now. She could become Ben's guardian! And she would take in Federico too, of course. She wasn't overly fond of the little Chihuahua, but she would do it for Lotti. And she and Ben would go to Pembrokeshire for the holidays with the dogs and rent a cottage near Lotti's school—better still, she and Ben would go and *live* in Pembrokeshire! And visit Lotti all the time!

Was this the life purpose she had longed for that night in London, after hearing about Max? To bring the children back and keep them safe?

Clara spent the evening packing. On Thursday morning, she took the train to London, and from there she went on to the coast.

Far away in Pembrokeshire, the secretary of St. Winifred's Academy entered the headmistress's study.

"It's about the new girl," she said. "Charlotte St. Rémy, the one who never turned up. I've telephoned every day, but nobody answers. Shall I write?"

"Yes, do," said the headmistress. "The usual letter for last-minute cancellations. Don't forget to mention the school fees."

The school secretary retired to her office and put a sheet of headed notepaper in her typewriter.

Dear Mr. Netherbury ... she began.

Chapter Sixteen

It was easy to pretend, between Monday morning when the *Sparrowhawk* and the *Starling* left Anfield Lock and Wednesday evening when they arrived in London, that they were on a sort of boating holiday. That Albert Skinner would not return, that the Netherburys would never discover Lotti's flight. That soon the *Starling* and the *Sparrowhawk* would not part ways, that the Thames and its currents, the murderous waves of the Channel, the waterways and battlefields of France did not lie ahead, with all their attendant dangers. Easy to pretend, as the sun shone down on the friendly, peaceful canals, that life could drift along like this for ever.

Lotti improved her driving and learned to operate locks. Ben perfected his handling of the *Sparrowhawk*. Federico, still enthralled by waterfowl but cured of swimming, took to sitting on the bow like a miniature figurehead.

Elsie slept.

And slept.

And slept.

By Wednesday morning, Ben was starting to worry.

"Do you think she's ill?" he asked Lotti when Elsie fell asleep straight after breakfast.

"Maybe she can sense something," Lotti replied. "Animals do, you know."

"Sense what?" asked Ben.

"Change," said Lotti. "It's all around us. Can't you feel it?"

It was true, the canal did feel different. Fields and villages were giving way to small towns, the lovely quiet waterways were growing more crowded. The crews of the boats they met were less inclined to chat but had an air of urgency about them as they hurried toward the capital, eager to offload their cargo and reload again before the day was done. Little by little, the sense of urgency communicated itself to Ben and Lotti, even Jim. Only Frank and Federico remained the same, one impassive at the helm of the *Starling*, the other inquisitive at the bow of the *Sparrowhawk*.

At midday, they stopped briefly for lunch. Rather

than watch hopefully for scraps as was her usual habit, Elsie lay on her side in the shade, breathing heavily.

"Look how swollen her belly is," said Ben. "Should I take her to a vet? How much would it cost?"

"A lot." Frank narrowed his eyes as he looked at Elsie.

"Never mind the dog for a minute," said Jim. "Me and Frank, we've been thinking. We'll be coming into Brentford this evening, so you two'll be wanting to catch the morning tide."

"What tide?" asked Lotti.

"The one on the *Thames*, Charlie," growled Frank.

"Oh yes," said Lotti, avoiding his eye. "I forgot about that."

"God give me strength," sighed Frank. "You *are* going to drown."

"We'll be unloading at Brentford Basin," said Jim, ignoring his brother. "And we was going to turn back, but what we're thinking is we'll see you on to the Thames first. Ben, you're first class at the tiller and Charlie, you've got a lot better, but the Thames is something different. You'll be heading east toward the sea, which means you got to cut right across the river to get in the right lane, and the current'll be fearsome. But all you got to do, Ben, is follow us and do exactly what we do.

We'll see you as far as Limehouse. After that, you're on your own. Happy?"

"Yes!" Ben swallowed, feeling daunted. "Very happy."

They woke Elsie, climbed aboard again and pressed on. Ben and Lotti's hearts beat fast, their breath was short, their palms were damp.

London!

The approach down to Brentford was steep, with eight locks over less than a mile, and the canal was busy. It was slow going, and hard work, and until they moored alongside the *Starling* in the crowded basin, Lotti and Ben paid little attention to their surroundings. When they finally looked up, they felt confused. They had been vaguely expecting packed streets, giant warehouses, throngs of smartly dressed people. They saw only a basin crowded with narrowboats, a boatyard, a handful of pubs and chandlers.

"It looks like any old town," said Ben.

"Go and look at the Thames if you don't believe you're here," Frank grunted. "Then you'll blinking know we're in London. And take that dog for a walk while you're at it, see if you can get her to drop before setting off on your blinking suicide mission."

He stomped away, hands deep in the pockets of

his patched jacket. Lotti and Ben watched him go, thunderstruck.

"Jim," whispered Lotti. "What does he mean, *get her to drop?*"

Jim scratched his head. "Lawks, this is awkward," he said. "Frank just worked it out, while we was coming down the locks. Elsie's pregnant, that's what. She's going to have puppies. And she's pretty far gone, I'd say."

"Puppies!" breathed Lotti, after Jim had gone.

"Puppies . . ." echoed Ben.

They looked at each other in awe.

"Do you think . . ." Ben tilted his head toward Federico.

"Of course," said Lotti. "Who else would it be?"

"It's a lot to take in," said Ben carefully. "I think I need to go for a walk."

"Yes," agreed Lotti. "Me too."

Side by side, with Elsie lumbering behind them and Federico trotting ahead, they headed away from the *Sparrowhawk* in the direction of the Thames, wrapped in thought.

Puppies! Lotti walked in a starry-eyed daze. Tiny little baby puppies! Soon—very soon, if Jim was right—they would be not just Ben and Lotti and Elsie and Federico living on the *Sparrowhawk* but a whole family . . .

How many of them? wondered Ben, chewing his lip. Would they be girls or boys? How did one look after newborn puppies? What did they need? And what if they came when they were out on the Channel? Would it be dangerous? What if something went wrong, and Ben was at the tiller, and couldn't help?

They had walked around the basin to the row of buildings on its southern edge and turned into a narrow alley between a chandlery and a pub. Something in the air changed as the light ahead grew brighter. The wind picked up, bringing with it a smell of river mud, laced very faintly with salt. At the end of the alley there was a wall, with steps leading up to the top. Lotti and Ben climbed them together, and gasped.

They had found the Thames.

As it flows east through London, the Thames at high tide swells as wide as four hundred and fifty feet at Woolwich. At Brentford it is still relatively modest, at about a hundred yards across. And though a hundred yards may seem a lot when you have been used to canals, it was not the size of the river that struck Ben and Lotti, but its strength.

Massive, gray, turbulent and sullen, the Thames pushed its way westward on the incoming tide, possessed of infinite energy.

There were steps on the river side of the wall, leading down to a strand of exposed mud and pebbles, about ten yards wide. Federico bounced down them. A gull landed in the water before him and was promptly swept away by the current. Federico, with a yelp of joy, gave chase along the strand.

Lotti burst out laughing.

"Come on, let's run!"

She tumbled down the steps after Federico to the edge of the Thames, and threw wide her arms to take a deep breath of salty, muddy London air. This was it—the end of the beginning, the start of the really big adventure! Tomorrow, the *Sparrowhawk* would take her place on this marvelous, powerful river, and all that was rotten about the past, Uncle Hubert and school bullies and pain and misery and loneliness would be swept away as surely as that gull.

She turned to Ben. "Isn't it wonderful?"

Ben had followed Lotti down on to the strand and was staring at the river in fascinated horror.

"Wonderful," he whispered.

"You're afraid," said Lotti, slipping her arm through his. "That's normal. It's huge, what we're about to do. But it's exciting too, Ben, it's *so* exciting."

"It is," said Ben determinedly. "And I'm *not* afraid. The Thames is just like a big canal, really. It's only *water*, and so's the Channel. We can absolutely do this. But I think I'll go back to the *Sparrowhawk* now. There's a lot to do before tomorrow."

He turned and walked back up the strand to the steps. Elsie lay on the wall, waiting for him. He crouched to pat her, and she gave his hand an affectionate lick as if telling him not to worry, then heaved herself after him down the street.

Lotti stayed on the strand a little longer and watched the Thames. Another gull sped past, bright against the filthy water, followed by the smashed remains of a barrel.

Ben was wrong. The Thames was many things—powerful, dirty, exciting, big—but it was nothing like a canal. Lotti thought back to childhood holidays, crossing the deep, heaving Channel with her parents to go to Armande.

The Channel was not *only water*.

Ben *was* afraid, whatever he said, and he was right to be.

After Ben had checked over every inch of the *Sparrowhawk* and made them both memorize her route again until they knew it by heart, they went to bed. Despite his nerves, Ben fell asleep almost immediately, but Lotti lay in her berth, listening to Elsie's heavy breathing from the floor in the galley where she slept with Federico.

Her hand closed over her father's ring.

"Bring us luck, Papa," she whispered.

But Lotti, who had lost her parents to a storm on a cloudless day, knew that the *Sparrowhawk* needed more than luck. She thought of Jack, Frank and Jim's little brother, who had taken a drawing of Nathan's starling with him to the war.

Rings and pictures were powerful things, but sometimes you needed *people*.

She waited a little longer until she was sure Ben wouldn't wake up, then climbed out of her berth, pulled on her clothes and, with Federico for courage, slipped away from the *Sparrowhawk*.

Chapter Seventeen

Lotti and Federico stood on the edge of the basin with the water behind them, facing the row of buildings that stood between them and the Thames.

Going to the pub, Jim had said, but which one? There were at least three.

"We'll have to try them all," she told Federico.

In all her life, Lotti had never set foot inside a pub. The first she came to was a soot-stained brick building. A man sat on a stool outside with a tankard in one hand and a pipe in the other, and stared curiously as Lotti went in. She squared her shoulders and pushed open the door.

The air was thick with smoke and the smell of beer, and the noise was deafening. In one corner, a group sang, huddled around a man bashing away at a piano. In another, a group of men were shouting, something to do with a bet, and money that someone did or didn't owe. Lotti stood with her back against the door and surveyed the room, eyes flicking from bar to piano, table to barstool. There was no sign here of Frank and Jim. She slipped away and moved on to the next pub, a low stone building. Here she found a quieter crowd, intent on a game of cards.

"What you after?" the landlord shouted as she peered in. "No kids allowed, and no dogs."

Lotti beat a hasty retreat. Frank and Jim were not here either.

It was properly dark now, and the dockside smelled of fish and coal and diesel oil. Lotti stepped over a bulk sprawled on the ground. The bulk groaned and she realized it was a person.

"I'm ever so sorry."

From the ground, something flew past her ear, only just missing her head, and crashed on the quayside in an explosion of glass and whisky fumes.

Federico growled. Lotti tugged at his collar and ran toward the third pub, straight into Frank who was strolling out with Jim.

"Should have known it was you when I heard trouble, Charlie."

Lotti peered back toward the drunk on the ground.

"I didn't *mean* to cause trouble."

"Course you didn't," said Jim. "Want a lemonade?"

"No, thank you. I've come to talk."

They sat on a bench outside the pub. Lotti waited as Frank lit his pipe.

"All right, then. What's this all about?"

"Ben's afraid." said Lotti, feeling like a traitor. "He says he isn't but I know he is, and so am I."

"Well, blinking hallelujah," grunted Frank. "You've come to your senses."

"Not exactly," Lotti hesitated. "More like I've come with a business proposition."

Frank's eyes glinted.

"Will you take us over?" Lotti asked in a rush. "To France, I mean? You said you know the Channel."

"I've never crossed it in a blinking narrowboat," said Frank.

"I'll pay you," said Lotti. "I don't have a lot of money, and what I do I rather need, but I was wondering if you might take this."

She pulled Papa's ring over her head.

Frank stared. "What is it?"

"It was my father's." Lotti fought to keep her voice level. "It's very old, and immensely valuable. I once heard my grandmother say it's been in the family since before the French Revolution."

Jim took the ring from Frank and whistled.

"It means a lot to me," Lotti continued. "But then so does getting to France. For . . . for all sorts of reasons."

Oh, Moune . . .

Frank smoked on and said nothing. It was Jim who spoke again, softly, using the same line of argument with his brother as on the day they helped to hide the *Sparrowhawk* from Albert Skinner.

"If it was our Jack, Frank, stuck in France . . ."

Frank's hand closed around the ring.

"I got two conditions."

Back on the *Sparrowhawk*, Lotti shook Ben gently by the arm.

"Wake up," she whispered. "I need to talk to you."

Ben turned on his side and looked at her sleepily. "Is it morning?"

"No, it's still night. I need to talk to you because . . . well, because I went to see Frank, because I knew you were worried, and I was too. And the good news is he's going to come with us all the way to France. You don't mind, do you?"

"No, it's good." Ben sounded relieved, and Lotti was glad. "But shouldn't we pay him?"

Lotti's throat tightened. "I've given him Papa's ring."

"The one you wear round your neck?" Ben sat up in his berth and looked at her, dismayed. Lotti had told him about the ring, and he knew how much it meant to her.

"I don't mind." It was a lie, but somehow the fact that she had had to give something up did make what she had to say next easier. "Ben, there's more. Frank says he'll only attempt the crossing if the weather's good. He says unless the conditions are perfect, the deal's off."

"Fair enough," said Ben.

Lotti gulped. "And he says . . . He says he won't make the crossing with Elsie. He says if something goes wrong it could put us all in danger, not just her, because you wouldn't be able to concentrate on the boat, and he wants two good pairs of hands on board, and I'm not good enough. And he's right," Lotti added honestly. "I'm not. Jim says he'll take care of Elsie. He says you can pick her up on your way back, when you've found Sam. *And* the puppies. But for now . . ."

"I have to choose," said Ben. "Elsie or Sam."

"Yes."

There was a very long silence, which Lotti did not dare interrupt.

"We'll leave her then," Ben said at last. "I choose Sam."

He managed to keep his voice steady but later, when Lotti was asleep, he crept out of his berth and called Elsie softly to him. Together, they padded into the workshop. They slept the rest of the night in Nathan's berth, with Ben's arms wrapped round his dog and his hands clutching her fur.

Chapter Eighteen

Lotti and Ben woke before dawn the following morning to a rap from Frank on the cabin hatch. For a moment, Ben forgot where he was. Then Elsie shifted beside him and he remembered.

He was leaving her.

"To find Sam," he reminded himself, but it still felt like a betrayal.

They had let the stove go cold overnight, to prevent sparks from flying if they hit rough waters on the Thames, and so it was a cheerless breakfast on the *Sparrowhawk* on the morning of their great adventure, bread and jam washed down with water and a hefty dose of heartache. All around them on the basin, other crews were waking, voices calling out to each other. On board the *Sparrowhawk*, dogs and crew sat in silence in the galley.

Another knock, then Frank swung down the steps, a rucksack over his shoulder.

"It's time," he said.

Ben, with a heart of lead, clicked his tongue. "Come on then, girl."

Very softly, Elsie began to whine.

"She's crying," said Lotti, close to tears herself.

"Rubbish," said Frank. "Dogs don't cry. Come on, Elsie. You'll have a grand time with Jim."

Still whining, Elsie backed into Nathan's workshop. Frank, with a groan of impatience, stepped after her and picked her up. Followed close behind by Ben, he carried her through the cabin and deposited her on the quayside.

"Lawks, she's heavy," he grunted. "At least without her we'll be lighter in the water."

Nobody smiled at his attempt at a joke. Jim folded Ben into a hug.

"Oh, for Pete's sake!" sighed Frank. "Don't tell me you're going soft too."

"It's a big thing, saying goodbye to your dog," said Jim.

But it really was time. Ben buried his face in Elsie's neck. Lotti, watching from the foredeck of the *Sparrowhawk*, tightened her arms round Federico. Federico whimpered. Elsie's whine turned into a howl as Ben, after a last caress, stumbled back onto the *Sparrowhawk*.

"Want to drive, son?" asked Frank.

Ben shook his head, incapable of speech.

Frank untied the moorings and fired the engine. As the *Sparrowhawk* pulled away, Ben kept his eyes fixed on the black and white figure on the quayside and saw, as Elsie strained against the lead, that the golden eyes he had loved since she was a puppy were watching him too.

He turned away so that no one would see him cry, then whipped back round at the sound of a yell from Jim.

His heart hammered. Elsie, her hefty weight notwithstanding, was galloping along the quayside, her lead trailing behind her. Jim, rubbing his arm, wasn't even trying to catch her.

"I don't blinking believe it," Frank said. "Not again."

"She bit me!" Jim shouted, but he didn't sound as if he minded. "She blinking bit me!"

Elsie was level with the *Sparrowhawk* now, gathering on her haunches, preparing to jump . . .

"Stay, girl, stay!" yelled Ben. "You'll hurt yourself."

Never underestimate a determined dog.

Elsie launched herself off the quayside as the *Sparrowhawk* pulled out of Brentford Basin and, to the cheers of half a dozen narrowboat crews, landed with absolute precision on the roof. When she had landed she lay down, panting, her eyes fixed on Ben as if to say, "Don't *ever* try to leave me again."

Laughing, or perhaps crying, Ben climbed up to join her.

"Good on you, Elsie!" yelled Jim. "Sorry, Frank," he added, seeing his brother's face.

But Frank knew when he was beaten.

"Get those blinking dogs in the blinking cabin." He pulled his cap more firmly over his smooth bald head, then, still grumbling, steered the *Sparrowhawk* into the lock and out again onto the Thames.

For as long as they lived, Lotti and Ben never forgot that ride through London.

The current leaped, tugging the *Sparrowhawk* sideways. The engine roared. Ben, who had chosen to stay below with the dogs because he couldn't bear to leave Elsie, sat on the floor with one arm round her and the other round Federico, holding his breath as he felt the hull beneath him shake. The dogs whimpered and pressed into him. Lotti, standing beside Frank at the tiller, gasped at the water's pull and tried not to think of the smashed barrel and the gulls swept away yesterday on the tide. But then, before any of them had time to be properly afraid, the *Sparrowhawk* reached the far side, Frank straightened up and they were off, no longer fighting the current but carried by it, flying into the sunrise. Lotti peered into the cabin and begged Ben to come and see.

"Look how beautiful," she said, as he came up the steps. "The sky, Ben! It's so much bigger than on the canals."

Out along the tree-lined river they swept, past the botanical gardens and under the bridge at Kew, sweeping round past Barnes and under the railway bridge to the suspension bridge at Hammersmith, under the stone pillars of Putney Bridge with its medieval churches standing guard at either end, under more railway bridges at Fulham and Battersea. After racing past the embankment at Chelsea, at last it felt like they were entering the proper city. They raced under Lambeth Bridge, and Lotti squealed as the Palace of Westminster came into view.

"We're going past the HOUSES OF PARLIAMENT!"

Lotti knocked into Frank as she jumped up and . down, and the *Sparrowhawk* briefly rocked as she veered off course.

"Sit down, Charlie, for heaven's sake," Frank shouted.

"BIG BEN!" Lotti screeched.

Frank's mouth twitched in an almost smile.

On and on they swept as the sun rose higher in the

sky and the light bounced off the water. Westminster, Blackfriars, Southwark. Lotti was counting off the bridges, using them to measure the distance between her and Barton.

"St. Paul's!" she squealed and then, in an awed whisper, "The Tower of London . . ."

The *Sparrowhawk* seemed very small, as they passed between the giant pillars of Tower Bridge. Ben felt a pang as he remembered another trip, long ago, looking up from the banks of the River Avon at the suspension bridge in Bristol with Nathan and Sam. Lotti, sensing his change of mood, reached out and hugged him. It was the first time she had done this, and he wasn't sure how to react. But then into his ear she whispered, "We'll get Sam back, just see if we don't. All four of us together, we can do anything," and he hugged her fiercely back.

Wider and wider the Thames swelled, until it was possible to imagine how it might turn into the sea. The city gave way to warehouses and docks, where giant cargo ships were anchored. Ben gulped at the sight of them. These were the boats they would see on the Channel, which could mow down the *Sparrowhawk* without even noticing . . .

"Anything," Lotti reminded him. "We can do *anything*."

At Limehouse, Frank turned a sharp right off the Thames and into the basin, and they all breathed out at the same time as the current stopped and everything slowed down again.

"That," declared Lotti, as the dogs scrabbled to be let out, "is the best thing I have done in my entire life."

Chapter Nineteen

At Limehouse, Elsie rested, Federico stalked seagulls and Frank went to discuss the weather forecast with the harbormaster. Lotti and Ben bought pies from a shack on the waterfront, and filled flasks with strong sweet tea for the next leg of the journey, out through the Thames Estuary and round the Kent coast.

"What'll we do if the forecast is bad?" asked Ben.

"Run away," said Lotti, licking gravy off her fingers. "Go by train."

"What about Elsie?"

"Leave her with Frank," grinned Lotti.

"Seriously, Lotti."

"It'll be fine," she told him. "Look at the sky! It's a perfect day for traveling. And here comes Frank looking really, *really* grumpy. That probably means he's had good news."

Lotti was right. Not only had the harbormaster confirmed an exceptionally calm forecast, he had also introduced Frank to the skipper of a Dutch barge, the *Wilhelmina*, which they could follow as far as Ramsgate.

"So everything is perfect," said Lotti cheerfully.

"Blinking marvelous," snarled Frank.

But even Frank's mood lifted as they rejoined the Thames. It was late morning, the tide was still with them, sunlight was bouncing off silver wavelets. Round the Isle of Dogs they went, past the Royal Docks and out toward Tilbury. The dogs stayed below, but Lotti and Ben and Frank all remained on deck, each taking turns at the tiller while the others drank in the surroundings. The river grew wider, its banks flatter and further away, the sky ever vaster, until it was almost possible to imagine what it might be like at sea.

"It reminds me of home," said Lotti when the city was quite gone and they were surrounded by marshes.

"Barton?" asked Ben, surprised.

"Not that home," said Lotti, and under her breath she began to sing, the song about the nightingale that Moune had taught her in her garden when she was little, which she had remembered on the night she rescued Federico from being shot.

"Pretty," said Frank. "What does it mean?"

"Oh, it's a very old song, and quite sad, but beautiful too. It's about a man who walks past a spring, and the water's so lovely that he swims in it, and then a nightingale sings and he says, *sing, nightingale, sing, since your heart is light.* But the man's heart isn't light, because his lover turned him away after he refused to give her a rose."

"Silly," said Ben.

But Frank, remembering a girl long ago whose heart he had lost for just such a foolish reason, said, "Teach it to us."

"What, in French?"

"Long journey ahead, Charlie. And French'll be useful where we're going."

And so Lotti taught them the song. And Frank and Ben struggled over the French, and they all laughed, but when she taught them the chorus, they all grew thoughtful, because the chorus went "*Il y a longtemps que je t'aime, jamais je ne t'oublierai,*" which means "I have loved you a long time and I will never forget you," and as they sang Ben thought of Nathan and Sam, and Lotti thought of Isobel and Théophile and Moune, and Frank thought of the girl he had lost all those years ago but mainly of his brother Jack, and the tide turned and the little *Sparrowhawk* battled on and her shadow on the water grew longer.

In the cabin, the dogs slept.

They turned eastward and the air grew sticky with salt. Ahead of them now there was only blue.

"Is this the sea?" asked Ben.

"Not yet," said Frank. "Still the Thames."

On they went, under that infinite sky until, six hours after leaving Limehouse, they reached the mouth of the estuary.

The first wave caught Ben by surprise, yanking the tiller away from him. The *Sparrowhawk* lurched. Lotti, who was making sandwiches in the galley, felt her stomach heave. Ben's blood flooded with panic. The dogs, jolted out of sleep, howled.

"Easy, lad." Frank's hand was over Ben's on the tiller. "Them waves aren't as big as they look, and the boat's stronger than you think. Hold steady. It'll grow calmer when we reach the open sea."

Steady, steady. The *Sparrowhawk* climbed up and slid down the swells but Ben, with Frank guiding him, felt the strength of the hull beneath his feet, the power of the engine driving them on.

"You said she'd sink at the first wave," Ben reminded him.

Frank said, "They're not real waves."

They reached the open sea and Frank was right, the

waves did calm. On and on they went, still hugging the coast, following the *Wilhelmina*, until all the tea was drunk and all the sandwiches eaten and all the light was gone. Lotti yawned, and Frank sent her below to sleep. The dogs were shivering on Ben's bunk. Lotti climbed in beside them and cuddled them. The *Sparrowhawk* rocked her like a cradle.

'*Jamais je ne t'oublierai . . .*' she sang to the dogs in a whisper.

I will never forget you . . .

Never

Ever

Ever.

Lotti slept.

A little later, Frank went below to use the privy, and for a few moments Ben was left alone at the tiller out on the darkening water, beneath a sky full of stars, and now something new was happening, something marvelous . . . The wake of the *Wilhelmina* and the wash of the *Sparrowhawk* swirled green with phosphorescence, and the two boats stood like jewels on luminous clouds in the oil-black sea.

"Magic," breathed Ben.

Out at sea, weather fronts were gathering, and far away inland, the train bearing Hubert and Vera Netherbury back toward Barton trundled through the night. But in that magical moment alone on deck, with nothing in the world but him and the boats and the sky and the waves and the strange otherworldly light, Ben knew that Lotti was right, and that he could do anything.

Chapter Twenty

The *Wilhelmina* left them at Ramsgate, headed to Nieuwpoort in Belgium. The *Sparrowhawk* stopped to wait for the next tide and to refuel, and for her crew to eat.

It was Friday morning, the weather was warm and already people were strolling about the waterfront. Breakfast at a nearby inn was plentiful and delicious. Frank, Lotti and Ben took their time over it. When they returned to the quayside, a small crowd had gathered around the *Sparrowhawk*.

"You never brought her round on the sea!" gasped a little boy holding a giant stick of rock.

There was no point lying about it.

"We *did*," said Lotti, proudly.

"The harbormaster says you're taking her all the way to France!" breathed the little boy's sister.

Ben pulled a face, but again, what was the point of lying?

"We *are*," said Lotti, and the little boy's and girl's eyes grew so round they looked like they might pop right out of their heads.

"Madness," said a man with a knotted handkerchief on his head, but he looked impressed.

A journalist from the *East Kent Herald* arrived with a camera.

"How long will it take you to get to Calais?" he asked.

"About six hours," grunted Frank, who didn't like crowds. "If everyone's finished chatting."

Lotti untied the mooring lines, and Frank fired up the engine. Ben put the dogs in the cabin, giving Elsie a special hug, then came back up and took the tiller. With Frank scowling at his side and Lotti on the storage box waving to the crowds on the quayside, he guided the *Sparrowhawk* out toward the open sea.

The journalist returned to his office to type up his story for the paper's weekend edition.

There was no *Wilhelmina* to follow now, no coastline to hug. Just forty miles of water ahead of them, the occasional cargo or military ship in the distance and the *Sparrowhawk* heading straight out to sea, alone. The dogs didn't like it. Elsie heaved herself onto Ben's berth and closed her eyes. Federico crouched beside her and looked accusingly at anyone who came in as if to say, "How much longer? How *could* you?"

But the sea was flat and the weather was fair and the *Sparrowhawk* was steady.

There was nothing to worry about.

Frank went below to rest, leaving Ben at the helm. Lotti stood beside him and breathed deeply. The air smelled of salt and engine fumes.

"Like freedom," said Ben, reading her mind.

"*Exactly* like freedom," said Lotti.

Softly, she began to hum the nightingale song and Ben joined in. But then there came a moment when England behind them disappeared, and France before them was still out of sight, and they stopped singing because the moment was too immense, and the only sound was the engine of the little *Sparrowhawk* bravely plowing on, slow and steady, slow and steady.

"We were so right to do this," said Lotti.

Ben smiled, and raised his face to the sun.

In silence, then, they continued, side by side, looking straight ahead. The tide turned and the going slowed but still the *Sparrowhawk* went on, and there was no reason to believe that anything would go wrong.

Little wavelets were breaking against the hull and the air was growing muggy, but the sky was still blue, the sea was still calm.

The French coast came into view, a white line on the horizon. There was a moment of jubilation, ecstatic and triumphant. Ben whooped. Lotti cheered. Frank stuck his head up out of the cabin and said, "Well, thank goodness for that. Want me to take over?"

"No way!" said Ben, and Frank went below again.

But, but, but . . .

A few moments later, Frank came back up, his expression grim.

"Blinking dog's started," he said.

Ben and Lotti stared uncomprehendingly.

"The puppies," said Frank, and took the tiller. "Go on." He sighed. "Go and see to her."

No, no, no! The puppies, now! This was what Ben had been afraid of! What if something went wrong? What if Elsie didn't know what to do? What if . . . Ben, with Lotti close behind, tumbled down the steps into the cabin.

Elsie lay in a tight ball on Ben's berth, with the blanket over her head.

She didn't appear to be in any discomfort.

"I don't understand," Ben shouted up to Frank. "Why do you think she's started?"

"Never seen a dog behave like that before," the answer came back.

"But I have ..." Lotti spoke in a whisper, her face very white. "She's doing exactly what she did when I first met you, Ben, when it rained so much even though it was a beautiful day. She's being a barometer."

They turned and climbed back up to the deck. In the short time they had been below, the temperature had dropped, the little waves grown stronger. France looked no closer, but the horizon had turned the color of a giant bruise.

"Look at the sky!" Lotti had said at Limehouse, not knowing these had been her father's exact words outside Barton Lacey all those years ago, when Isobel wanted to stay.

Storms.

Sometimes, it seems, they come from nowhere.

The *Sparrowhawk* was pitching all her power against the tide now, and the tide was winning. The air was cold, the sky lowering, the sea still calm, but it was different from the calm before. Then the sea had felt asleep. Now it was swelling, gathering strength. And it was no use wishing for the peaceful canals, the green tranquillity of the English countryside, the relative safety of the London Thames as they flew into the sunrise, the calm coastline and the comforting presence of the *Wilhelmina*. All the *Sparrowhawk* crew could do was hold their course, and pray that they would reach safe harbor before the storm broke. Frank held the tiller now. Ben stood at his side. In the cabin, Lotti tried to comfort the panicking dogs.

Minutes passed, which felt like hours. Inch by fought-for inch, the French coastline grew closer.

"Calais," breathed Frank at last, pointing to a white shape in the distance, more guessed at than seen.

The current had swept them off course. Frank brought the *Sparrowhawk* round to hug the coastline, heading east. Ben saw cliffs, trees, a church, and he willed the boat on faster.

The waves grew.

"No worse than the ones we had yesterday," said Frank.

But the waves swelled higher. Lotti, her arms wrapped round the dogs, gave a moan. Federico was sick. Elsie burrowed deeper into her blanket.

The first drop of rain hit them within sight of the Calais harbor walls, followed almost immediately by a flash of lightning that ripped open the sky, then by a rumble of thunder. With a sudden, vicious gust, the wind whipped up. With an answering heave, so did the sea.

"Ben, go below," ordered Frank. "Get a bucket and give it to Charlie. Tell her to go into the workshop and watch the foredeck. She's to stay inside except if a wave breaks over the bow, in which case she's to bail for all she's worth. And tell her, if the *Sparrowhawk* goes over, to get the hell out and hang on to the hull and not let go, whatever happens. Whatever happens, you hear? She's to climb on top of it, if she can."

"What about the dogs?" Lotti whispered, pale-faced, when Ben delivered Frank's message. "What'll happen to them if the *Sparrowhawk* goes over?"

"She won't go over," said Ben, handing her a bucket from the galley.

"But what if she does? *They* can't hold on to the hull, they'll drown … And Ben, what if the *Sparrowhawk* sinks?"

"She won't go over and she won't sink," Ben repeated stubbornly, but the *Sparrowhawk* was lurching badly now, and he almost fell as he came back out onto the deck.

He saw Frank's face before he saw the wave. Frank the unmovable, strong, silent, dependable Frank was pale as a ghost, mouth open, eyes staring, frozen to the spot—still holding the tiller, but no longer steering.

Ben turned to follow his gaze.

Monstrous, the wave towered over the *Sparrowhawk*.

The little boat lurched again. Below deck, the dogs howled, Lotti screamed. Up above Frank froze with fear, but Ben didn't hesitate. He pushed Frank out of the way, seized the tiller and drove straight into the wave.

Chapter Twenty-One

The *Pride of Kent* passenger ferry had seen many storms in her time, and this was definitely one of the worst. Most of the passengers in the first-class lounge had spent the Channel crossing groaning in their club chairs. As the coast of France hove into sight, the swell of the waves grew to the size of a townhouse. A small girl was sick in an ice bucket. Her brother followed, then their governess. Two elderly gentlemen gagged and staggered out to the deck, only to be swept back in seconds later by the howling wind, one of them without his hat.

Seated at the bar before a cup of coffee, only a splendid young man with hair the color of newly ripened chestnuts and a patch over his left eye remained unfazed. His name was Captain Henri de Beauchesne, and in his four years of war service in the French navy he had seen much worse than people being sick in buckets. He spent most of the voyage reading the newspaper, but glanced more and more often toward the deck, where a young woman stood peering over the railings.

She had been there since the *Pride of Kent* set out. Henri had assumed at first that she was seasick, but about halfway through their journey she had looked up and he had changed his mind. The woman wore a deep frown, and even from a distance he saw that she was chewing her lower lip. It was not the look of someone about to heave their lunch into the Channel.

Intriguing, thought Captain de Beauchesne, sipping his coffee. It did not occur to him to interfere. But then the swell that had undone the small children and their governess grew again. Henri's coffee flew out of his cup, the saucer crashed to the floor. The children threw up once more, their governess screamed and inexplicably sprinkled them with lavender water, and one of the elderly gentlemen lurched toward the bathroom with his hand over his mouth.

Out on deck, the woman was flung to her knees.

Henri raced to help her.

The *Pride of Kent* rolled one way. Henri reeled the other. The heavy deck doors swung back in his face, but with a nimble twist he avoided them. The sea spat salt spray at him. He ignored it and skated elegantly across the rain-slicked deck toward the young woman.

By the time he reached her, she was already back on her feet and leaning over the railings.

"Madame, come away!" he shouted. "It is not safe!"

She turned toward him.

The wind blew, the sea swelled. The storm raged and the rain fell. Inside the lounge, the second elderly gentleman sprinted for the bathroom. Henri de Beauchesne was aware of none of these things. Stars exploded in his mind. His heart danced in his chest. The world was reduced to the vision of a pale face framed by swirling red hair, a pair of large gray eyes behind small round spectacles.

The vision spoke. Henri strained forward to listen.

"The children," she whispered.

Henri looked wildly about the deck. He could see no children.

"Please," he said. "Tell me how I can help."

"Not here!" she cried. "Out there!"

Clara Primrose flung her arms toward the sea and burst into tears.

At Barton Lacey, Hubert Netherbury opened the letter from St. Winifred's, in which the school secretary informed him that Lotti had not arrived, expressed hope that all was well, and reminded him that the deposit he had paid to secure her place was non-refundable.

It was difficult to determine, in the roar that followed, whether Hubert was more angry at having been made a fool of again, or because he had paid money for nothing.

But he was definitely furious.

For the second time in a week, he telephoned the police.

"Find her," he said.

PART III

Chapter Twenty-Two

The *Sparrowhawk* crew were wet, cold, elated, trembling, torn between triumph and tears. The cabins were awash with seawater, the decks were slaked with rain, the dogs were damp and cross, but they had done it! They had beaten a storm, and they were alive! Safely secured to the harbor wall, they waited to go through customs before making their way inland.

With shaking hands, bitterly ashamed of having frozen out at sea but weak with relief that Ben had saved them all, Frank pulled his passport from his rucksack, and told Ben and Lotti to do the same.

"Oh," said Ben.

Frank looked at him suspiciously. "What now?"

"I don't have one," said Ben simply.

Frank swore.

"I sort of forgot," Ben admitted. "I've never been abroad before."

Lotti, who was cuddling the dogs on Ben's berth, cast Frank a reproachful look. "We just survived a storm in the Channel, Frank. I think we can manage a customs officer. Ben, what papers *do* you have?"

Embarrassed, Ben produced the documents he had found before leaving Great Barton—Nathan's passport, the *Sparrowhawk*'s papers, his own birth and adoption certificates. Lotti bit her lip in concentration as she went through them.

"I think," she announced, "now would be a good time to lie."

When customs officer Jean Lepage arrived, they were ready for him, though their hearts sank when they saw him, because he looked even grumpier than Frank.

Which, right now, was saying something.

Frank, with a grimace that was meant to be a smile, produced Nathan's passport and the *Sparrowhawk*'s papers. They all held their breath as Jean Lepage inspected them, and tried not to look too grateful when he handed them back.

"The children?"

Lotti handed him her passport. Jean raised his eyebrows.

"You are not his daughter," he said in French. "And you are not English."

Lotti, beaming from ear to ear in the mistaken belief that it made her look relaxed, replied that Frank was a dear family friend, and that she was French on her father's side, though her *maman* had been English.

"Where are they now, your parents?"

"Dead," said Lotti.

Jean Lepage flushed and turned to Ben. Frank produced Ben's birth certificate. Jean Lepage's eyebrows rose again. Frank produced Ben's certificate of adoption.

"My son," he said, his voice admirably steady.

"And his passport?"

"Doesn't have one," said Frank, avoiding the officer's eye. "No time. Had to leave in a hurry."

Jean Lepage's eyebrows disappeared into his hairline. Lotti flew to Frank's rescue. "Monsieur Langton is bringing me to the funeral of my grandmother," she said in French. "She died so very suddenly. Of influenza. Ah, *grand-mère*! How I loved her!"

She wiped an invisible tear from her eye. Frank, not understanding a word, looked alarmed. Jean Lepage asked, "Would it not have been easier for him to bring you on the boat train?"

"But Monsieur Langton *has* a boat!" Lotti cried,

looking astonished. "*This* boat, which he lives on with Ben! Who is his son! Why would we take the boat train?"

"It is most irregular," Jean Lepage grumbled, and Lotti was beginning to despair, and wondering whether she should not just throw herself on his mercy and tell him the whole truth, when from the workshop where they had put the dogs there came a yowl of pain. Ben opened the door, and Federico shot through the cabin into the safety of Lotti's arms.

"What happened?" she cried.

"I think Elsie bit him," said Ben, looking into the workshop. "She's growling and she just bared her teeth at me."

Jean Lepage rubbed his face and, wearily, asked to see the dogs' papers.

"Ah," said Lotti.

How well, she wondered, would this glum-faced official respond to the story of Federico's rescue from Malachy Campbell?

"She's started!" Ben shouted. "Elsie's started!"

Lotti squealed. Frank gazed at the ceiling. Would this help or make things worse?

"*What* has started?" asked Jean Lepage.

"Puppies!" breathed Lotti.

Jean Lepage gave up. So the boy had no passport? He seemed happy enough. So the people on the

Sparrowhawk were eccentric, possibly mad? This was not a reason for not coming into France. Frankly, thought Jean Lepage, feeling a sneeze coming on, the world had bigger problems.

"Through the harbor to the basin, there is a lock at the far end on the right which will take you on to the canal. Please leave immediately, there are more boats coming in. Welcome to France."

The sneeze caught Jean on the quayside by the *Sparrowhawk*, and he stopped to blow his nose. Putting his handkerchief away, he remembered Lotti's face as she told him there were puppies. It had worn a look of pure wonder. When, after all these years of war, had he last seen that?

Throughout the day, whenever he thought of the *Sparrowhawk*, Jean Lepage smiled.

Back on board, Lotti was feeling triumphant.

"See how right we were to bring Elsie?" she said to Frank. "Clever dog! *Perfect* timing!"

"All right, all right," grumbled Frank. "Here, take these blinking papers. I never want to see them again."

With a wide grin, Lotti took the documents and shoved them into a drawer in the galley. Then, with infinite care, Frank steered the *Sparrowhawk* through the busy harbor toward the lock, while in the cabin,

Ben and Lotti hovered with Federico by the door to the workshop.

"Where's Elsie?" whispered Lotti.

"On the berth," said Ben. "She's made a sort of nest, like she did before the storm."

"How do you know it's not another storm nest?"

"It's just different."

"Can we look?"

"Maybe we should leave her . . ."

"But I want to see . . ."

Very quietly, so as not to disturb Elsie, Lotti and Ben tiptoed into Nathan's workshop, Lotti with her hand on Federico's collar . . .

Frank guided the *Sparrowhawk* under a rotating bridge and through the lock. About a hundred yards on, he saw a small hotel set back from the canal, with mooring rings in the bank. He stopped and secured the *Sparrowhawk* and went into the hotel to speak to the hotelier, a fierce but friendly widow called Madame Royère. Then he ordered a coffee and a sandwich, sat down and wrote a note.

The door of the workshop was half open when he returned to the *Sparrowhawk*. In the gray light of the fading afternoon, he saw the outlines of the children kneeling on the floor with Federico, Elsie on the berth. Lotti looked up and saw him.

"There are three puppies already," she whispered. "You'll have to take one, Frank, when they're big enough and can leave Elsie."

"I'd like that." Frank smiled.

Lotti turned away. He watched them a while longer, then picked up his rucksack from where he'd left it in the galley, tucked his note into the fold-down table and left the *Sparrowhawk*.

Chapter Twenty-Three

Ben found Frank's note when he went into the cabin to light the stove for tea after the fifth and final puppy was born. He brought it back into the workshop to Lotti, and they read it together kneeling by Nathan's berth.

I'm not one for goodbyes, as you might guess. But I wanted to thank you. If you'd told me a week ago I'd be crossing the Channel on a narrowboat, I'd have said you were daft. But you've shown me what's possible, and you've reminded me what's important too. So I'm not going back to England just yet. Jim can take care of the Starling. I'm going north to Belgium instead, to find Jack's grave. The

*landlady of the hotel knows you're here and
will help with anything you need . She speaks
English and I told her something of your story.
She's very impressed. She should be.*

Frank

PS: the hotel is called La Belle Ecluse.
*Apparently, that means the beautiful lock.
Sounds better in French—like your song,
Charlie.*

"It's very *him*," said Lotti, after she and Ben had read it
together. "I mean, I can't imagine him saying goodbye,
it's true. And it's a very kind note. Beautiful, really. And
I'm glad he's going to Belgium. But I'll miss him."

"And now we're alone." Ben swallowed, thinking
of the task ahead without Frank's solid presence beside
him.

"Not *exactly* alone," laughed Lotti. "Not with seven
dogs! Oh, Ben, *look* at them! Their little squashed noses
and their little pink feet! And isn't Elsie clever? She
knows exactly what to do."

Lotti leaned with her elbows on the mattress, gazing

in rapture at the five tiny creatures, four black and one toffee, stumbling and clambering over each other as Elsie licked them clean.

Federico climbed into Lotti's lap and nuzzled her neck jealously.

"You're clever too," she whispered, hugging him. "The four little black ones are just like Elsie, but the tiny toffee one is going to be exactly like you. Look, she even has your ears! I'm going to call her Delphine, because it means dolphin and she was almost born at sea."

"You can't tell it's a girl yet," objected Ben.

"I *can*," said Lotti. "I *know*. What shall we call the others?"

Ben looked round the workshop for inspiration. His eyes fell on the collection of Dickens novels in the bookcase, which Nathan had read out loud to him and Sam, over and over for years.

"Pip," he said. "From *Great Expectations*. And Dodger, of course, from *Oliver Twist*, and Fred from *A Christmas Carol*, and Boz, which was Dickens's own nickname. Do you think we can touch them?"

He reached out a hand to Elsie, as if asking her permission, and she licked it. Very gently, he laid a finger on the soft warm body of one of the black puppies and caught his breath.

"I can feel its heartbeat ..." Then, with a touch of sadness, "I wish Nathan could see this."

"But he can," said Lotti softly. "They all can—Nathan and Mama and Papa. They're right here watching with us. Can't you feel them?"

They sat very still, hardly breathing, so that in the workshop the only sound was the puppies' mewling and the steady beat of rain on the roof, and Ben *could* feel it, something magic in the air like you get in very old churches, or libraries, or empty houses which people have really loved.

"I have to tell you something," Ben whispered to Lotti. "It sounds mad, but on the boat, when I drove into that big wave, I thought I heard Nathan speak to me."

"What did he say?" asked Lotti.

"He said, *Steady, lad, you're doing fine,* just as he always used to, and then I felt ... I felt his hand on my shoulder. *Does* that sound mad?"

Lotti smiled.

"Come on," she said. "I want to show you something."

Ben followed Lotti through the cabin up onto the rear deck. Ignoring the rain, Lotti climbed up onto the roof, followed by Federico.

"What are you doing?" Ben called up. "You'll get soaked!"

"Who cares!" she shouted back. "It's only water! Ben, look around you!"

Ben looked. What was he supposed to see? There was a canal, twice as wide as those at home, poplar trees, a lock—the hotel Frank had written about, square and white with faded gray shutters and bright geraniums at the window . . .

He began to smile.

"France, Ben!" sang Lotti. "We're in France!"

He climbed up to join her on the roof. Lotti grabbed his hands, and they began to jump up and down shouting, "We're in France! We're in France!" with Federico leaping around them barking, not caring that they were getting soaked because Lotti was right, it *was* only water, and together they had taken on the world, they had beaten Hubert Netherbury and Constable Skinner and a wild, wild storm.

No one could stop them now. No one!

Two figures appeared on the towpath, a man and a woman, hunched against the rain. Ben and Lotti paid no attention. The figures drew closer. Lotti stopped jumping, then Ben.

The figures stopped and the woman looked up, and it was Clara with a man they didn't know.

Thunderstruck, soaked, Ben and Lotti stared.

"You mad children!" Clara cried. "Get down from there at once!"

Then she burst into tears again.

Clara had prepared a speech but for a while, as she sat on the berth with Lotti and Ben standing before her and Captain de Beauchesne hovering uncomfortably in the galley near the door to the workshop, all anyone could make out were snatches of sentences as she sobbed.

"I thought you were drowned . . . I was so frightened . . . I thought you were dead . . ."

"But we're not dead." Lotti sat down beside Clara and patted her hand. "We didn't drown. Clara, how did you know we were here?"

"We asked the harbormaster," said Captain de Beauchesne, when Clara failed to answer. "It was not difficult to trace you. You already have quite the reputation in Calais."

He had meant it as a compliment and was unprepared for the consternation which greeted the news that, once again, they had failed absolutely to be inconspicuous.

"What I actually meant," said Lotti, "is how did you know we were in France?"

"Martha . . ." sobbed Clara. "Her sister, Molly . . ."

"Molly!" Lotti hissed.

She looked apprehensively toward the hatch. "Did Molly tell anyone else? Clara, have *you* told anyone else?"

Before Clara could reply, Captain de Beauchesne in a stunned voice said, "There are puppies. Rather a lot of them, on the berth in this room at the back. I heard growling, so I looked."

The surprise finally made Clara stop crying. "Puppies?"

"Elsie's," said Ben. "And Federico's."

"But I didn't know she was ..."

"Neither did we," said Ben.

"Clara!" said Lotti. "Answer the question! Have you told anyone where we are?"

"I have not," said Clara. "Oh, Lotti, your *hair*!"

Lotti let out her breath. "So why are you here?"

Clara, finally, launched into her speech. She was still very emotional, and they had to concentrate hard to understand what she was saying. It involved cottages in Pembrokeshire, and guardianships and looking after dogs—although possibly not a whole litter of puppies, she said, floundering at this unexpected obstacle. But the general gist, as they understood it, was that Clara had come to look after them, and take them home.

"Because, Ben, dear, about your brother—you do

know how difficult it will be, don't you? How very, very difficult, I really mean *impossible* . . ."

She faltered under Ben's glare.

"It is *not* impossible," Ben said. "We've got a plan, haven't we, Lotti?"

"We have." Lotti got up to stand beside Ben. Federico, sensing a threat, left the galley, where he had been keeping a suspicious eye on the captain, and trotted across the cabin to join them.

"We are *not* going back to England," said Lotti.

Henri de Beauchesne started. Until now he had been enjoying himself. The storm, the rain, Clara . . . Children lost, children found. Puppies, and this extraordinary boat, and its unlikely crossing . . .

But now, this talk of England . . .

Henri observed the scene before him. The girl and boy, ragged, damp, filthy, the absurd small dog. They looked, he thought, like a small but fierce combat unit. For his own private reasons, Captain de Beauchesne mentally joined their ranks.

If Clara went back to England now, how could he be sure to see her again?

"Please," he begged. "Allow me to be of assistance."

Chapter Twenty-Four

Four years in the navy had turned Henri from a dreamy boy into a ruthless organizer.

"To begin with," he declared, gazing round the damp, steaming cabin of the *Sparrowhawk*, "you cannot stay here."

And he took himself off to La Belle Ecluse, the little hotel by the lock, where he booked three bedrooms—one for himself, one for Clara, and one for Ben and Lotti, with stalls full of fresh straw in the stables for the dogs.

Lotti and Ben tried to resist, but it was impossible.

"Federico will be lonely," protested Lotti. "Elsie's not really talking to him now she that has the puppies, and what about the horses?"

"There are no horses," Henri replied. "They were all requisitioned by the government for the war. Madame

Royère has bought a car instead. And dogs are not permitted in the bedrooms."

"But what if the *Sparrowhawk* gets stolen?" Ben worried.

"She will not get stolen," Henri promised. "But she is damp, and that is not good for humans or for little dogs. Also, the blankets on which Elsie had her puppies must be washed, no?"

This was undeniably true.

"Madame Royère will see to the washing," Henri continued. "And she will not charge for your mooring. She is very admiring of your exploits crossing the Channel. I told her, Ben, that you have come to France to look for your brother, and she regards you as a sort of hero."

"Great," grumbled Lotti. "The whole world knows about us."

"The chambermaid, who was in love with an English soldier, has also offered to clean the *Sparrowhawk* for free."

"No." Here Ben put his foot down. "The *Sparrowhawk* is my boat. I don't want anyone meddling with her."

Henri, ever the naval man, said that this he could understand, and he would cancel the maid, but that he had arranged for dinner to be served in the hotel dining room at half past seven.

"And don't tell me you would rather eat on your boat," he said, anticipating Ben's next objection. "The smell of Madame Royère's cooking is a thing to make you weep for joy. I have looked in your pantry and all you have is soup. Please, you are my guests. This is your first night in France. It is to be properly celebrated."

Dinner was a stew of rabbit cooked in red wine, served on a bed of buttery mashed potatoes. Afterward there was an alarmingly smelly, round, runny cheese which Ben eyed warily until he saw Lotti smear it onto pieces of crusty French bread. The cheese was followed by an apple tart so light and delicious he wondered if he had ever truly eaten dessert before. During the meal, Henri asked Ben and Lotti to explain their plan for finding Sam, and listened carefully as they told him how they aimed to take the *Sparrowhawk* to the site of the hospital-bombing near Buisseau, and to interview the farmer who had known Nathan, in the hope that he could tell them something about where Sam was taken, and to visit neighboring hospitals.

"And when will you leave, on this brave quest?" asked the captain.

It was kindly meant, but Ben and Lotti bridled at the indulgent tone.

"As soon as we're ready," said Ben. "I need to

check over the *Sparrowhawk* after the storm, and buy provisions, and also plan our route. Most likely the day after tomorrow at first light."

"Well, I wish you luck." Henri raised his glass. "To a heroic journey! And to new friends."

He smiled warmly at Clara, who blushed and looked away.

Later, when Ben and Lotti were lying in their trim twin beds in a little bedroom under the hotel eaves, Lotti said out loud what they were both thinking.

"He doesn't believe we can do it, does he?"

"No," said Ben. "He's just trying to impress Clara."

Lotti propped herself up on an elbow to look at him. "Do you think he's in love with her?"

"Maybe. But it's awfully quick. I mean, they've only just met."

Lotti lay back down and looked thoughtfully at the ceiling. "Does that matter?" she asked. "People do fall in love at once. Just like I knew as soon as I met you that we were going to be friends."

"I don't know. She looks sad."

"She always looks sad," said Lotti dismissively. "Ben! I've just had an awful thought—do you think they're going to want to come with us?"

"He might be helpful," said Ben. "Frank was."

"We needed Frank," said Lotti. "We don't need him

or Clara. He'll just flounce about giving orders to impress her, and she'll keep telling us we really ought to go back to England."

Ben twisted round to look at her. "You're cross with her," he said.

"No, I'm not," scoffed Lotti. "I'm just being practical. It's going to be hard enough doing what we have to do without dragging around people who don't believe in us. We'll have to tell them they can't come."

There was a short silence in which they both tried to imagine telling Henri and Clara they weren't wanted, then Ben said, "Lotti?"

"What?"

"Just now, you said it was going to be hard. I do know that. Just in case you thought I didn't. But we will find him. I can feel it."

"Course we will," said Lotti. "We just beat a blinking storm. Finding Sam'll be nothing compared to that."

Ben fell asleep and dreamed of wind and waves. Lotti stayed awake much longer. She thought about Ben and how he would feel if they didn't find Sam, and she thought about Clara and her garbled speech on the *Sparrowhawk*. From what Lotti had understood, Clara wanted to rescue Ben from going to an orphanage and have him live with her, but she had said nothing about rescuing Lotti.

"But that's all right," Lotti whispered into the dark. "When Sam's found, I can rescue myself. It's not as if anyone can stop me."

At Great Barton, Albert Skinner cycled wearily home from Barton Lacey, where he had been interviewing Zachy about Lotti. Zachy had told him nothing of any use. Tomorrow, Albert would go to Kent to interview the maid Sally, whom Hubert Netherbury had fired, but who had likely been the last person to see Charlotte St. Rémy before she vanished.

At Ramsgate, the *East Kent Herald*'s printing presses whirred.

Chapter Twenty-Five

Bright sunshine followed the storm. Ben and Lotti came down to breakfast in rebellious moods, ready to inform Captain de Beauchesne and Clara that they would be continuing their journey alone, but neither of the adults was there.

"The *capitaine* left an hour ago on a motorcycle which belonged to my cousin, who can no longer ride it because he has only one leg," said Madame Royère, as she served them hot chocolate.

"Captain de Beauchesne has only one eye," Lotti pointed out.

"For riding bicycles, one eye is better than one leg," said Madame Royère. "He has gone to make inquiries for you, poor children."

"What sort of inquiries?"

"*Ah, ça.*" Madame Royère shrugged. "I don't know. And Mademoiselle Clara is sick. Well, she is crying, and has kept to her room. I know this sickness. It is a sickness of the heart. Also, you must take the father dog for a walk, he has been crying all night. So many dogs! Already I have had to chase away all the town children who want to see the little English puppies who were born on a boat."

At the stables, Federico greeted Lotti with frenzied reproach. Elsie thumped her tail and allowed the children to admire the puppies. The four little black puppies were feeding gustily and already appeared bigger than yesterday, but toffee-colored Delphine was just as tiny, and mewled pitifully as she tried to push in past her siblings to feed. Lotti picked her up, kissed her and tucked her in close to her mother. Then, with Federico on a lead, she and Ben went into town.

Ben gazed around curiously. Calais looked tired, like the *Sparrowhawk* two months ago when he came back to live on her, faded and battered and in need of paint and repair, but it was exciting to be here. Ben jumped aside at the loud clanging bell of a tram, he stared up at the tall narrow houses with shuttered windows. They walked past a café. He breathed in the smells of tobacco and coffee, and felt his blood run a little faster.

"It's so different from home," he said.

"It's certainly shabbier than I remember," mused Lotti, sidestepping an overflowing dustbin. "I expect that's the war, like in England. Or maybe it's just that I was seven when I was last here. There's a lot you don't notice when you're seven."

The first thing they bought in town was a map, which they studied on the street outside the shop.

"I reckon two days to get to the hospital site," said Ben. "So we'll buy provisions to last at least that. Once we're off, I don't want to stop again except to sleep."

"Let's find food supplies, then," said Lotti. "I'll ask someone. Oh, Ben—look!"

She took his arm and dragged him across the street to a *pâtisserie*, with a dazzling array of cakes in the window.

"*That's* not shabby!" she said. "Come on, I'm going to buy you an éclair."

"Lotti, there's no time for cake!"

"Ben!" Lotti was shocked. "There is *always* time for cake!"

In a little square shaded with sycamore trees by the *pâtisserie*, while Federico stalked pigeons, Ben and Lotti sat on a bench to eat their cakes. Biting into her chocolate éclair, Lotti felt the years peel back. She was seven years old again, sitting with Papa in a café in the market square at Armande on the last day of the holidays, and he had bought her a cake as a treat.

"Don't tell Moune or Mama," Papa had said, with a twinkle in his eye. "You know how they feel about eating between meals."

"It spoils the appetite for lunch," seven-year-old Lotti had recited, hollowing the cream out of her éclair with a finger.

Oh, those summer holidays! And if Lotti were to eat cake in Armande again, would it taste the same without Papa?

She's different here, thought Ben, watching Lotti. More French, like this was where she belonged, just like he belonged on the *Sparrowhawk*, but also more restless, like she was searching for something.

For the first time, it occurred to him that Lotti had never spoken of what she would do once they had found Sam.

They returned to La Belle Ecluse laden with parcels for the journey, and spent the rest of the day working on the *Sparrowhawk*. By the time Henri de Beauchesne returned late in the afternoon, the narrowboat's interior was gleaming again, and the clean bedding was drying on the hotel's washing line. Lotti and Ben were scrubbing the outside, watched from the roof by Federico, and by red-eyed Clara from the steps of the hotel. They all gathered on the towpath to hear what the captain had to report, Lotti noting with interest that Clara stood a little apart.

"After much discussion with various parties," said Henri, "I have worked out the route you must take which will bring you closest to the site of the bombed hospital at Buisseau."

He produced a copy of the same map Ben and Lotti had bought in town that morning, and showed them his proposed route. It was identical to the one Ben had worked out, except for its final destination.

"I had thought to bring the *Sparrowhawk* right up to the hospital site," Ben said. "Nathan wrote in his letter that barges went there."

"Unfortunately, I have been informed that the river to that site is now unnavigable. Which is why I suggest this . . ." Henri pointed again at the map. "Here, at the intersection of these two rivers, there is a convent where the religious sisters nursed many soldiers during the war. They are good women, and I am sure they will help us. By my calculations the convent is a little more than a day's journey away from here by boat. Then it is about twelve miles to Buisseau by train from the local station of St. Matthieu."

Lotti, irritated, admitted to herself that this *was* helpful.

Henri turned to Clara. "I will ride ahead,

Mademoiselle Clara, and alert the good sisters of your arrival."

Now was the moment, thought Lotti.

"Tell them," she whispered to Ben. "Say we don't want them to come!"

"Why me?" he whispered back.

"It's your boat!"

"I don't know what to say." Ben was gazing at Captain de Beauchesne in stupefaction. "He's so ... efficient."

"All right," said Lotti. "I'll do it."

But she didn't have to.

"Captain," said Clara, in a voice that only shook a bit. "Could we talk?"

Henri and Clara walked together along the towpath away from the hotel.

"You are so kind," Clara said, when they were out of hearing of the *Sparrowhawk*.

"I'm not sure I am," Henri replied honestly. "I'm not sure I should be encouraging Ben to search for his brother. It seems to me a quite hopeless endeavor. What is your English expression? A needle in a haystack."

"Yes," said Clara. "You're right, of course. But I'm awfully afraid he needs to find this out for himself."

"Mademoiselle Clara ..." Henri de Beauchesne blushed, uncharacteristically bashful. "The reason I am helping . . . Everything I have done, I have done for you. I must tell you . . ."

"Oh, please don't!" said Clara.

"You don't know what I am going to say!"

"But I do!" Clara was close to tears again, but she also wanted very much to explain. "The thing is, I have just lost—there was this boy, this young man, I loved him so much, and waited for so long, and now . . . I have just learned that he is dead, and I don't even know if I *can* love anymore. I don't even know if I still loved *him*—the feeling had become so mixed up with the feeling of waiting. Even my family, my parents—they disapproved of him so strongly, they threw me out of their home. I have been so removed from love for so long, I think I've forgotten what it is. So you see, I cannot—I mean, it would be unfair—I mean, I cannot ask you to help us more than you have already so very, very kindly done."

"Even as a friend? Even if I don't mind that you don't love me?"

"Even so." She tried to smile, but it hurt too much.

Henri looked across the canal to where a clump of daisies on the opposite bank danced in the afternoon breeze. He had a mad notion that he would like to wade across to pick them for her. But then he thought that the gesture would embarrass her, and also that she was the sort of person who probably preferred flowers to be left alive. He felt a surge of anger toward anyone who might hurt her.

"May I ask—if it is not too indiscreet—why your parents disapproved so much of the young man you loved?"

Clara sighed, and he worried that he had offended her. But then she spoke again, very softly.

"He was German," she said. "But it didn't matter to me, and it shouldn't matter to them."

And then she left.

So much said, so much left unsaid. Clara, hurrying away from Henri along the towpath, wished she had the courage to go back to tell him that in another life, in other circumstances, she might have given him a different answer. He, recovering from her revelation, wanted to call out after her that Max's nationality didn't matter to him either, and that he would wait for her, just as she had waited for Max.

And also something else.

"You are wrong," he wanted to tell her. "You say that you can't love, but you can. You love those children."

But Henri didn't speak, and Clara didn't go back.

Henri watched the water a little longer, then returned to the hotel by a different route, paid for all three rooms, spoke briefly with Madame Royère and left on her cousin's motorbike for Paris, where he lived.

Lotti and Ben watched Clara walk listlessly back toward the *Sparrowhawk*.

"Oh dear," said Lotti. "Ben . . ."

"I know," he said. "We can't leave her."

"We can't, can we? Poor old thing, she looks so miserable. *Someone* has to look after her. Do you think she'll mind sharing Nathan's workshop with the puppies?"

Chapter Twenty-Six

At last, they were going to find Sam!

The *Sparrowhawk* left La Belle Ecluse at first light on Sunday morning. The canal was wide, flanked by crops of ripening corn and barley, and there were foxgloves and meadowsweet on the banks. The weather was kind, sunny but not hot. In the workshop, in a blanket-lined fruit crate, Elsie nursed the puppies, and at his favorite post on the bow, Federico clocked ducks, songbirds and kingfishers. The scene was peaceful, almost idyllic, but among the crew the mood was tense. Ben at the helm was in a trance, focused entirely on driving, the only way he could control his nerves. Seated on either side of him on the storage boxes, Lotti and Clara, understanding his need for silence, were lost in their own thoughts—Clara of what she had left behind, Lotti of what lay ahead, at Buisseau, where they would look for Sam, and beyond that for herself . . .

About an hour out of Calais, something deep inside the *Sparrowhawk*'s hull began to rattle.

"Shouldn't we check what that is?" Clara asked.

"It's nothing," said Ben.

"It doesn't *sound* like nothing . . ."

"We're not stopping until we find Sam."

Shortly after lunch, they turned inland and came to a small town, where any sense of idyll was lost completely.

This, then, was what a country looked like after a war.

The town had been destroyed. The church was missing a roof. Most houses were missing walls. Over a shop, a once jaunty *pâtisserie* sign hung jagged above a hole where the door had been. And the trees . . .

"They've all been cut down," said Lotti. "Why?"

"They got in the way of fighting," said Clara.

Max had written to her of this once.

"The poor trees . . ." Lotti thought of the beech alley at Barton, the woods where the nightingale sang. The fate of the trees upset her more than anything. "They were just *there*. *They* didn't choose to go to war."

"Nobody chooses to go to war," said Clara.

"Somebody must," said Ben. "Or it wouldn't happen."

They sailed on, quiet but for the rattle of the *Sparrowhawk*.

Later that afternoon, in a meadow surrounded by wildflowers, they saw the shell of a fighter plane. Lotti, thinking of her parents, heaved over the edge of the bow. Clara went to comfort her but Lotti pushed her away, and sat frozen for some time holding Federico, staring unseeing at the landscape which looked so similar to landscapes she had visited with her parents, and yet which felt so different.

In the early evening, they passed a graveyard. It was a war cemetery, and it was not clear from the canal to which country it belonged, but it seemed to stretch for miles, grave after grave, some older, some freshly dug, each marked with a wooden cross. Ben cut the engine, and the *Sparrowhawk* drifted in silence interrupted only by the song of birds and the faint rustle of the breeze in a nearby copse, and they all thought the same thing but didn't say it—that crossing the Channel had been child's play compared to finding Sam in the midst of such monumental destruction.

They moored for the night under some poplar trees, by a field where brown cows grazed. They ate cold chicken and an apple tart given to them by Madame Royère, and they cuddled the puppies, but not even the soft sweetness of the little dogs could erase what they had seen. Later, when Clara had gone to bed in Nathan's workshop, Lotti reached her hand down from her berth. Ben stretched up to hold it and they lay like this for a while, awkward and uncomfortable but not wanting to let go.

"So many graves," whispered Lotti at last. "It seems . . ."

"Impossible," said Ben.

"But we'll find him, Ben. You just see if we don't."

Ben squeezed her hand, then whispered, "Your parents. The plane. Lotti, I'm sorry. I'm sorry I brought you here."

"You didn't," said Lotti. "It was my idea, remember? We brought each other."

Eventually it grew too uncomfortable to keep holding hands, and with another squeeze they let go, though neither could have said who let go first.

"It will be all right," said Lotti. "As long as . . ."

" . . . we're together," said Ben.

They both wondered, as they drifted off to sleep, when they had started to finish each other's sentences.

On Monday morning, at about ten o'clock, they reached the lock that led from the canal to the river on whose banks stood the convent Henri had told them about, where the good sisters had nursed soldiers during the war. It was a relief to leave that canal, with its somber memories. The river was lined with trees, and if there were horrors beyond them, at least they were hidden from view. And there was something different about being on a river instead of a canal. Rivers felt alive, thought Lotti, waiting at the tiller for Ben to return to the *Sparrowhawk* from the lock. This particular river was slow and lazy. It didn't have the force of the Thames, or its sense of grandeur, but the feeling was there, an implicit invitation to come and play.

One day, Lotti promised the river, we will. But not yet.

They both had so much still to do.

"Ready?" she asked, as Ben stepped back on board.

"Ready."

Ben squared his shoulders and gazed straight ahead.

The *Sparrowhawk* rattled on toward the convent.

Sally had denied all knowledge of Lotti's whereabouts when Albert interviewed her. She hadn't seen Lotti since the night before the poor kid left for school, when she begged not to be waved off the next morning, because she didn't want Sally to see her cry.

After the interview, Albert had missed the last train back to Great Barton, and spent Saturday night in a room above a pub. As he waited for his train on Sunday morning, he picked up a copy of the weekend edition of the *East Kent Herald*. His heart skipped a beat. On the third page, under the headline PLUCKY CHILDREN HEAD FOR THE HIGH SEAS, was the photograph the journalist had taken of the *Sparrowhawk* in Ramsgate harbor, with Ben at the helm and Frank and Lotti beside him.

In detective work as in life, luck will play its part.

Back at Great Barton, Albert Skinner went straight to Barton Lacey to inform Hubert Netherbury of his discovery.

"I don't understand." Lotti's uncle stood in Théophile's study with the newspaper in his hand, staring at the photograph. He did not invite Albert to sit. "What is this boat? And who are these people?"

"I don't know who the man is," Albert admitted. "The boy, of course, is Ben Langton."

"Who?"

"The lad who has been sharing lessons with Charlotte . . ." Albert faltered under Hubert's glare. "It's his boat. I'm sorry, sir, I assumed you knew . . ."

"Well," said Hubert through gritted teeth. "I didn't."

Glowering, he stared at the wall behind the desk, then frowned. The painting which hung there was ever so slightly lopsided . . .

≈ ≈ ≈

Albert left for France on Monday morning, with orders to drag Lotti back to England if he had to, but to do it discreetly. As the train pulled out of the station, he thought how curious it was that through all his conversation with Hubert Netherbury, not once had the man shown any concern about his niece's safety, only outrage at her behavior. Well, the girl had certainly made a fool of her uncle—running away, nicking diamonds, not to mention getting him to pay for Ben's education, and the strange business with Malachy Campbell's dog . . .

As for Ben, stringing Albert along for weeks about his brother . . .

He remembered the day he had told Lotti and Ben they had to go to school—even then, they had been defying the rules. They were a force to be reckoned with, those kids, no doubt about it.

But then, so was Albert Skinner.

PART IV

Chapter Twenty-Seven

Ben's heart was in his mouth, and Lotti's too, as he brought the *Sparrowhawk* alongside the convent's rickety jetty. It was a lovely place, the river slow and lazy and fringed with trees, with dragonflies skittering over the surface and house martins flying low to drink. But it was also the place where the search for Sam on the water ended, and the search on land began.

They had not realized, until they stepped ashore, how safe the little narrowboat made them feel.

"The dogs should stay," said Clara. "We don't know if they're welcome."

"The captain said they were good women," protested Lotti.

"That doesn't mean they like dogs."

No boat, no dogs . . . Ben and Lotti suddenly felt

very exposed, but they walked side by side with quick determined steps along a path which led from the jetty to a faded door in a high wall. It opened with a creak when Ben pushed it, and the travelers stepped inside.

They found themselves walking in long grass in an overgrown orchard. On their left, a row of apple trees showed advanced signs of blight, and when the house came into view they saw that several of its shutters were broken, and that unchecked ivy grew thickly on the walls. And yet despite this, there was a solidity to both house and orchard, as if the breeze rustling through the trees and the ivy were whispering, *times have been hard, but we are still here . . .*

"It will be all right," Lotti whispered to Ben. "I have a good feeling."

A bench had been placed by the back door, which was open, and from inside the house came the sound of a woman singing. Clara stepped forward, calling out a greeting in French. Immediately the singing stopped. An elderly nun came to the door, wiping her hands on the apron she wore over her gray habit, and introduced herself as Sister Monique.

"And you are the English travelers!" she said, with a smile.

"We are," said Clara, with a surprised laugh. "But how did you know?"

"There was a telegram," said Sister Monique. "From a *capitaine*."

Clara blushed. "Captain de Beauchesne?"

"Yes, perhaps. I did not see it myself. But the Reverend Mother said that when you arrived, we were to bring you straight to her."

A little bewildered, the travelers followed Sister Monique out of the kitchen and down a passage to another door which led them into a pleasant parlor with views over the orchard, where a tall, stately woman wearing the same gray habit as Sister Monique rose to greet them and introduced herself in careful English as Mother Julienne, and asked how she might be of assistance.

The Reverend Mother listened attentively as Ben and Lotti told her of their plans. When they had finished, she joined her hands together as if in prayer, and looked at them thoughtfully. She was a kind woman but known for her plain-speaking, and for always telling the truth.

"It will not be easy," she said. "To find a person missing for so long, after such a war as this . . . it is almost impossible. But you must know this already. Here is what I can do for you. There is a mission house in Buisseau, closely affiliated to ours. Sister Monique stays there sometimes when she goes to Saturday market. I will give you a message to take to them. You may stay there while you conduct your search, and they will help you."

"Thank you," said Ben. He spoke calmly but his heart was hammering. "We'll leave immediately. How do we . . . how does one get to Buisseau from here?"

"The railway station at St. Matthieu is twelve miles away. Sister Monique can take you in the pony cart. You may leave your boat at the jetty; it will be quite safe. You will all be going?"

"The puppies," said Clara. "Someone ought to stay with them. Lotti . . ."

"Absolutely not," said Lotti. "I'm going with Ben."

"It would be better if you went with an adult," said the Reverend Mother. "Buisseau, that whole area—it has suffered much."

"I want Lotti," said Ben. "It doesn't work if we're not together."

He and Lotti stepped closer to each other, until they stood shoulder to shoulder facing the two women. Looking at them, Clara and the Reverend Mother had the same feeling that Henri de Beauchesne had experienced on the *Sparrhowhawk*, of seeing a small, efficient combat unit.

An hour later, after a quick lunch, Lotti, Ben and Federico left for the railway station. Clara stayed behind to look after the *Sparrowhawk* and the puppies.

≈ ≈ ≈

How strange, thought Ben as the train pulled out of the station, that after all they had been through, this last stage of the journey should be so straightforward. He spent the train ride with a local map borrowed from Sister Monique spread over his knees, tracing and retracing the route between Buisseau and the river. His breathing was short and painful. Three miles, about an hour's walk from the station at Buisseau, and he would see the last place where Nathan had been alive, and he would speak to the farmer he had stayed with, and he would ask where exactly the survivors of the bombing had been taken and maybe, maybe, tomorrow they would find Sam.

He tried not to think about what it would be like, out there close to where the bombs had fallen.

Lotti, sitting beside him with Federico on her lap, heard Ben's shallow breathing and watched him trace the map, and thought, Please, please, please let it work.

It was mid-afternoon when they got off the train. As the Reverend Mother had warned them, Buisseau had suffered in the war. The station was dirty, its platform still being rebuilt after suffering shelling. On the main square, there were gaps where once there had been houses, and several shops were boarded up, with FOR SALE signs stuck to the boards. But in the southwest corner, Lotti glimpsed a café terrace ... Was this where she had once stopped with her parents on their way to Armande and drunk pineapple juice?

She thought of the sycamore-shaded square in Calais where she had sat with Ben, remembering the time Papa had bought her a secret cake.

How would pineapple juice taste now?

Lotti longed to find out, but she was also afraid ... And anyway, Ben did not want to linger, and right now she was here for him. They did not even stop at the mission house to leave their rucksacks, but set out immediately toward the river, following the map.

Chapter Twenty-Eight

Nathan had described his lodgings in one of his many letters home, which Ben had kept preciously and knew almost by heart.

> *It's hard to be here, so near the front, with the noise of the guns and the night sky all lit up from the artillery fire. To be honest it sounds like hell, and I pity the poor people caught up in it, all the more so since I've seen your brother. But the farm where I'm staying is like a paradise. I don't mean the sort of paradise you read about in books with angels and harps and all that, more a quiet paradise on earth, with turtledoves cooing in the woods and tubs of red geraniums and a weathervane on the*

*roof in the shape of a fox. It's called Chez
Thibault. That means Thibault's house,
and it's been Thibault's house for nearly
two hundred years, having been built by the
current owner's great-grandfather . . .*

Lotti and Ben left Buisseau on a raised road flanked
on both sides by fields. After walking almost two miles
through gentle farmland, they noticed that the fields
around them had become dotted with ponds and pools,
which reflected the sky, filling the landscape with light.

"Pretty," said Lotti. "But why so much water?"

"Shell holes." Ben swallowed. "And there are no
trees."

"Oh," murmured Lotti. "I see."

They walked on, their footsteps steady and their eyes
straight ahead, feeling increasingly uneasy. About forty-
five minutes after leaving Buisseau, they came to a track,
where a small sign indicated that they should turn off for
Chez Thibault.

"We're nearly there," said Lotti. "The place where
Nathan stayed."

"Yes," said Ben, almost inaudibly.

The place where Nathan stayed, the farmer Nathan
stayed with . . .

He knew before they even reached the farmhouse

that it would be terrible. *Turtledoves cooing in the woods*, Nathan had written—but the woods were blown to bits, and all the birds were gone, and the farmhouse was destroyed.

Lotti reached for Ben's hand and held it tight. Together they advanced toward the ruins. A piece of metal stuck out of the ground at an awkward angle by an old well. When they drew near, they saw it was the weathervane in the shape of a fox.

"They must have come back," whispered Ben. "The bombers. After they hit the hospital, after the farmer wrote to me."

"I'm sorry," whispered Lotti. "Oh, Ben, I'm so sorry . . ."

What could she do, to take away his grief? What had helped her, all those years ago after her parents died? Queen Victoria the cat, and Moune, before she disappeared . . . Being held, being loved . . . She glanced at Ben. His face was ashen. Should she hug him? She wanted to, but then he squared his shoulders in a way that suggested he didn't want to be touched.

"I think," he said very carefully, "that I would like to go to where Nathan died."

They walked on to the site of the field hospital, but there was little left to show of the lives of the doctors and nurses and ambulance drivers and orderlies and patients and men who had passed through. In the burnt remains of a hut, Ben found a blue and white teacup. In a grassed-over shell crater, Lotti found a tobacco tin. In the hole left by an uprooted tree, Federico unearthed a boot.

They went on to the river, and saw why it had become unnavigable, as Captain de Beauchesne had told them. A few hundred yards upstream, its banks had collapsed in the bombing, and trees had been blasted across the water, creating an unpassable barrier that, for now at least, had been left to rot.

This was what they were aiming for, thought Ben. Not the hospital—the river. And then, This is where Nathan died. Why aren't I upset?

He searched himself quite carefully, looking for appropriate emotions, but felt nothing but a terrible numbness. After a while, realizing there was nothing for him here, he said they should leave. They walked back along the raised road. The evening sky reflected in the ponds and pools and ditches was the color of blood.

In a lonely corner of the Protestant cemetery, they found Nathan's grave, his name and date of death roughly carved on a plain wooden cross. Ben stood before it for a long time, still numb, but forcing himself to remember. Nathan, the first time Ben and Sam had met him, with Bessie and his soft hat, bandaging Ben's foot . . . Nathan, who had painted him a robin, Nathan teaching him to read, to write, to pilot the *Sparrowhawk*, Nathan, who had loved him and Sam like sons ... Little by little, the memories forced their way through the numbness, and Ben sat down right there on the grave and sighed, but still he did not weep.

Lotti, watching from a discreet distance with Federico, felt that her heart might break.

I shouldn't have suggested this, she thought. Just because I wanted to get away—I wanted to come to France—but I should have thought. I shouldn't have put him through this.

At last, Ben turned away from the grave.

"Let's go back to the *Sparrowhawk*," whispered Lotti. "Let's go back to Clara and Elsie and the puppies."

But Ben's jaw was clamped in a way she had not seen before, and his features had hardened into fierce, stubborn resolution.

"We're not going back," he said. "Just because the farmer is gone doesn't change anything. Other people can tell us which hospital the survivors were taken to. It's still the same plan. We'll sleep at the mission house and then tomorrow we'll go to the hospital and see if Sam is there, and if he's not we'll ask to see their records to find out if he ever was there, and we'll also ask everyone, *everyone* if they've seen Sam. We'll show them his photograph, just like you said, and we won't leave until someone recognizes him."

"Ben . . ."

"Don't tell me it's impossible. I know we can do it, I can *feel* it. We'll find Sam. We'll find him, because we have to. I can't lose him as well as Nathan, I can't."

Back on the *Sparrowhawk*, Elsie was restless, prowling between the puppies and the deck, sniffing and whining. Clara tried to calm her.

"Ben'll be back soon," she promised, stroking her. "And he'll never leave you again, don't worry. I'll make sure of that."

Long after night had fallen, Elsie settled. The black puppies rushed to feed, pushing little Delphine out of the way. Clara picked her up and placed her closer to her mother, then prepared herself for bed. When she was ready, she climbed into her berth and pressed her forehead to the window above it to look at the shadowy woods and river.

It looks like a fairy tale, thought Clara.

Suddenly, for a moment, she froze. Then with a shaky laugh she let out her breath.

She could have sworn she saw a face, watching the *Sparrowhawk* from the trees, but it was only the reflection of the moon on the water.

Chapter Twenty-Nine

The sisters at the mission house were kind. It was plain that they didn't believe in Ben's quest any more than the Reverend Mother, but they were helpful. Sister Marianne, who was in charge of the mission house, told them that survivors from the bombing had been taken to a civilian hospital in the nearby town of Rainvilliers, about ten miles away. Sister Angèle, the cook and a friend of Sister Monique's, made them sandwiches and found them bicycles. Ben and Lotti set off as soon as they had finished breakfast, leaving a resentful Federico with Sister Angèle.

The hospital was a square, white modern building on the outskirts of Rainvilliers. Ben and Lotti locked their bicycles to a railing and went inside, and Lotti explained what they had come for to a tired-looking receptionist. The receptionist didn't look surprised by their request, or even sad, but directed them to a room, which had been set aside especially for people like them.

Their hearts sank as they came into the room. They had arrived early but already it was full. A stern-faced woman at a desk by the door gave them a numbered ticket and told them to wait until it was called to see the official record-keeper.

"Why are there so many people?" asked Lotti.

The stern-faced woman looked at her pityingly. "Even now, all this time after the war, half of France is looking for a missing loved one," she said, "and *you* are searching for an Englishman!" she added, as if Englishmen were famously the most difficult to find.

All the chairs in the room were occupied. Ben and Lotti shrugged off their rucksacks and found a space on the floor to sit and wait. Lotti stole a look at Ben and was alarmed to see that he was shaking.

"Maybe it won't be so long," she said, slipping an arm through his.

"It's not the wait," he whispered. "It's ... we're *here* ..."

"And soon we'll know," said Lotti. "Yes. It's scary."

Ben sighed and briefly rested his head on her shoulder, then gave himself a shake and reached into his rucksack for the envelope in which he had put Sam's photograph.

"Take it," he said, giving it to Lotti. "There's no sense both of us waiting in here, and your French is better than mine. Go and ask people if they've seen him?"

Lotti took the photograph and examined it carefully.

It was a formal shot, taken in a studio before Sam left for the war. He wore an army uniform and his hair was cut very short, but his mouth was twisted in a half-smile, his eyes were crinkled and there was a dimple in his left cheek. The guardians of the orphanage would have had no trouble recognizing the boy they used to define as trouble. "What a laugh!" the face in the picture seemed to say, as if he wanted Ben and Nathan to remember him as he had always been, rather than what he was about to become.

"I like him," said Lotti.

Ben's mouth trembled. "So do I."

"I promise," said Lotti, "if anyone here remembers Sam, I will find them!"

She hugged him and hurried out of the room.

Ben waited.

There were double doors at the back of the room. As numbers were called, people got up and went through them. All sorts of different people were here. An old farmer in his Sunday best, a woman in a dark silk dress, a young man with a stick. They all went in looking nervous. They never returned smiling.

Lotti started outside the service doors of the hospital, watching the porters unload crates from a truck, feeling strangely nervous and un-Lotti-like, because she remembered the cold hard look on Ben's face at the river yesterday, and at Nathan's grave, and she wanted very much to make that look go away.

"*S'il vous plaît*," she asked one of the porters when he stopped for a cigarette. "*Regardez! Avez-vous vu cet homme?*"

Please, look! Have you seen this man?

It was not the first time the porter had been asked this question, in this manner. He had never yet recognized a face, but nonetheless he took the photograph and examined it. Called over his colleagues, who also looked. Handed it back, as he always did, with a sorrowful shake of the head.

"*Non, désolé.*"

I'm sorry, no.

Nurses, kitchen staff, doctors, orderlies. Cleaners, ambulance drivers, even patients. Lotti moved to the main entrance and showed the photograph to every person who passed.

Mainly, she drew blank looks. Sometimes, a sorrowful shake of the head. Once, a hug.

But nobody recognized the photograph.

The morning passed. Lotti came in to take Ben's place so he could go outside to stretch and use the bathroom. He came back and ate his sandwiches. He closed his eyes and found that by focusing really hard on his breathing, he could slow down his heart and pretend he wasn't there. In out in out. He opened his eyes and saw that the afternoon sun cast long shadows across the floor, and thought with a fierce longing of the *Sparrowhawk*.

Lotti came in from outside, looking exhausted. Most of the chairs were free now, but Ben still sat on the floor. Lotti flopped down beside him.

"Nothing?" he asked wearily.

"Nothing."

Four o'clock came, and the records office closed at five. They began to lose hope of ever being called, but then . . .

"*Numéro soixante-trois!*'

Number sixty-three!

They jumped up, with their hearts in their mouth.

Their turn had come.

≈ ≈ ≈

"It will be difficult, at the hospital," Sister Angèle had told them before they left the mission house. "You will see things, what war does to people."

Lotti had replied, "But we have seen that already, all the time, everywhere. The servicemen at home who came back from the war with bits missing, Captain de Beauchesne who lost his eye. And we have seen the villages which were destroyed, and the farmhouse, and the cemetery with thousands of graves."

"The hospital will be worse," said Sister Angèle.

The door to the ward opposite the record-keeper's office had been wedged open to create a draught. And in the end, the record-keeper had to repeat himself twice before either Ben or Lotti heard what he said.

Afterward, they walked out of the hospital into the hot still afternoon, gripping each other's hands. Sam was not at the hospital, and the register held no record of him, but this was not the reason they held on so tight.

Sister Angèle had been right.

What they saw on that ward was much, much worse than anything they had seen before.

Chapter Thirty

Albert Skinner was in Calais, interviewing customs officer Jean Lepage.

Had Jean Lepage seen the *Sparrowhawk* come through? He had! Albert Skinner was relieved. Where had the *Sparrowhawk* gone? It was very important. The children on board had run away, the girl's uncle was looking for her and the boy was an orphan with no family.

Jean Lepage found himself in a dilemma.

On the one hand, he knew the stories circulating in Calais about Ben and Lotti. If there was the slightest chance of the boy finding his brother alive, he had no intention of getting in their way. His own nephew had disappeared at the Battle of Verdun, his sister had spent months scouring hospitals for him. Also, there was the memory of the girl's face when she told him about the puppies, that look of wonder, which Jean had not forgotten.

On the other hand, one did not lie to policemen.

Jean Lepage compromised.

"Try asking at La Belle Ecluse," he said. "The landlady there may be able to help."

Madame Royère had none of Jean Lepage's scruples about lying. Henri de Beauchesne had given precise instructions before he left about what to say to anyone who came looking for the *Sparrowhawk*, and promised to reward her for saying it.

"They have gone to Paris," the landlady said firmly, and gave Albert the captain's address.

Albert had one final question, about something that had been troubling him since he left England.

"Tell me," he asked. "With the children, were there dogs?"

Madame Royère rolled her eyes. This was a subject dear to her heart.

"So many dogs!" she sighed. "Puppies!"

"Puppies?"

"Five!" she told him. "Four black like the mother, the fifth a toffee-colored runt, with the ears of her terrible father, who cries all night."

So Malachy Campbell's Chihuahua had made it to France, thought Albert.

"Thank you, madame," he said.

He left for the station, to catch a train to Paris. As soon as he was gone, Madame Royère telephoned Captain de Beauchesne, to warn him of the policeman's arrival.

Henri sent a second telegram to the convent, this time addressed to Clara, hoping that she was there, that it would be helpful and, most of all, that she would be pleased with him.

Sister Monique brought Henri's telegram to the *Sparrowhawk*, noting with interest that Clara blushed as she read it.

```
POLICEMAN ARRIVED BELLE ECLUSE . . .
STOP . . . ALBERT SKINNER . . . STOP . . .
ROYERE TOLD HIM YOU ARE IN PARIS,
FOLLOWING   MY   INSTRUCTIONS   . . .
STOP . . . WILL DEFLECT AND INFORM YOU
OF  FUTURE  POLICEMAN  ACTIVITY  . . .
STOP  . . .  PLEASE  LET  ME  KNOW  IF  I
CAN ASSIST FURTHER . . . STOP
```

"What should I do?" asked Clara.

"About what?" asked Sister Monique drily.

"About the policeman, of course."

"The captain tells you that he will deflect him. Is it so bad, if the policeman finds you?"

Yes, thought Clara bleakly, it is so bad. And yet, at some point, wasn't it inevitable that the law would catch up with them? What would happen now? In the unlikely event that Ben found Sam alive and well, he would live with his brother, but if he didn't? For the first time, Clara realized that in haring after the *Sparrowhawk* with no plan other than to keep Ben and Lotti safe, she had actually made things worse for them. Would anyone allow her to become Ben's guardian, now that she had helped him run away? And would she herself be in trouble with the law? She wasn't sure where it stood with respect to Ben, but she was fairly sure it would take a dim view of the fact that she hadn't returned Lotti to her uncle.

She should have insisted on bringing Lotti home before the Netherburys returned from Scotland, taken her to St. Winifred's, begged them to say nothing of the late arrival to her uncle ... Hubert Netherbury would be furious. Clara had met him only once, when he interviewed her to tutor Lotti, but she had a fair idea of the sort of man he was. Suddenly, she felt very afraid for Lotti.

Oh, she should have done everything differently! And yet Clara also knew that nothing she said could have stopped Ben and Lotti, and that had she given them away, they would never have forgiven her.

Sister Monique was asking her a question.

"Do you trust this captain?"

Clara thought about the efficiency with which Henri had helped them at La Belle Ecluse, his bashfulness toward her at the end. Unconsciously, she stroked the telegram with her thumb. She knew that Henri would keep Albert Skinner away for as long as he could.

After that, who knew?

"I do trust him," she said.

"Then save your worry for the children," advised Sister Monique. "Or, better, pray for them."

Her eyes fell on the puppies nestled with Elsie in their crate.

"The little toffee one is too thin," she observed.

"I know," said Clara. "I keep trying to help her feed, but Elsie is so unsettled since Ben went away, she doesn't seem interested."

"Bring her to the kitchen," suggested Sister Monique. "I've some fresh goat's milk, we'll try her with that."

As they walked up to the convent, a gardener came toward them pushing a wheelbarrow. He stopped and straightened to let them pass, and Clara felt a small shock. She had seen him several times from a distance and had assumed from the way he carried himself that he was an old man. Close up she saw that he was quite young, though his ragged clothes and thick beard and the livid scar that ran down his left cheek from his temple made it hard to guess his age.

"A poor lost soul," sighed Sister Monique when they were out of earshot.

"Who is he, and how did he get that scar?"

"Nobody knows, because he does not speak. He appeared earlier in the spring, and the Reverend Mother took pity on him and gave him work. He lives in a cabin in the woods. We call him Moses, because he loves to watch the river."

"Poor man," said Clara, but she shivered as she followed Sister Monique through the orchard, feeling the gardener's eyes still on her, and remembering her feeling last night on the *Sparrowhawk*, that she was being watched then too.

Chapter Thirty-One

"We'll go to every house between the hospital site and Buisseau," said Ben at breakfast on Wednesday. "We'll show them Sam's picture and ask if they saw him."

"Every house?" Lotti paled.

"Every single one," said Ben. "Also in Buisseau itself. People don't just *disappear*. *Someone* must have seen him.'

Since the hospital, Lotti had known that it was hopeless and that they would never find Sam this way. It had been a brave, defiant plan, but all the adults had been right, it was impossible. Ben refused to see it. Well, Lotti could understand that, and she still felt the responsibility of having suggested the plan in the first place, so she would continue to support him, but she felt profoundly weary. After what they had seen yesterday at the hospital, Lotti almost hoped Sam *hadn't* survived. To be alive, and look like that . . .

She tried to shake the image out of her head. It was no good thinking like this, no good at all.

Leaving Federico once again with Sister Monique, Lotti and Ben cycled all day through the countryside between Buisseau and the river, on tiny roads to knock on the doors of remote cottages and farmhouses, on tracks down to where laborers worked in the fields, down paths to visit gamekeepers and woodcutters . . .

"I'm sorry to disturb you, mademoiselle, have you seen this man?"

"Monsieur, I am looking for an English soldier . . ."

People cried, people sighed. People closed doors in their faces, people invited them into their homes. Over cake and grenadine, they showed Lotti and Ben their own photographs and told their own stories, but no one remembered Sam.

They returned to Buisseau in the late afternoon. Ben wanted to continue the search in town, but Lotti couldn't go on.

"I'm so tired," she said.

Ben was angry with her, and Lotti truly was sorry, but all through the day, as the terrible sad stories of the war piled up, her mind had kept returning to the café in the southwest corner of the main square, which she had glimpsed on Monday when they came off the train.

She wanted, very much, to sit there quietly and remember, and discover if she had the courage to do what she had come to France to do.

Lotti left Ben and cycled toward the town center. When she reached the main square, she dismounted and wheeled her bicycle to the café.

The late-afternoon sun was still warm, and the terrace outside was beginning to fill up. Lotti loitered, suddenly shy, still holding her bicycle.

"What do you want?" an elderly waiter came out of the café and barked at her.

"I'm just looking," she stammered.

He gazed at her suspiciously. In the glass of the café window, Lotti caught sight of her reflection and understood. The old shorts and jersey pulled from the Barton jumble pile, already stiff with salt from the Channel crossing and stained with oil from the *Sparrowhawk*, were thick with dust from the day's cycling. After a week living on the water, her face was tanned as a sailor's and she hadn't had a proper wash since La Belle Ecluse. She looked like an urchin. Uncle Hubert and Aunt Vera would be appalled.

The thought gave Lotti a deep satisfaction.

"Do you have any pineapple juice?" she asked the waiter.

"Not had that since the war," he said firmly.

"Grenadine, then. I've got money, I can pay."

"We don't have grenadine either."

Every café had grenadine, it was one of the most basic things you could ask for, but Lotti didn't argue. The waiter didn't want her here, and Lotti wasn't even sure this was the café she had come to with her parents anyway. It looked similar, but that could just be her memory playing tricks on her. It certainly didn't feel the same.

Later, though, when she was asleep, she saw that day again clearly in a dream—Mama sitting in the sun in her white dress, Papa in his straw hat, even the glass of pineapple juice. But then the glass exploded and turned into the burnt carcass of an airplane. Lotti woke weeping in the small hours and did not go back to sleep.

"Monsieur, I'm sorry to disturb you, this is a picture of my friend's brother . . ."

"What's that, girl? Give it here, I can't see, my eyes aren't what they used to be . . ."

Lotti and Ben spent all of Thursday knocking on doors through the streets of Buisseau, on foot this time, dragging Federico on the lead, with Ben obstinately optimistic and Lotti privately despairing. By the end of the afternoon, the photograph was in a sorry state, worn thin with handling, the gloss of its surface dulled by strangers' fingers. Clumsily handled by an old man with poor eyesight, it fell apart. Back at the mission house, Ben tried to repair it, but glue only made it worse. Sam's face was ripped in two, and completely unrecognizable.

"You can still tell it's him," Ben insisted. "*I* can still tell it's him. We can describe him."

But now Lotti and Sister Angèle and Sister Marianne all said, "Enough."

Ben folded his arms on the table, and laid down his head, and closed his eyes, and didn't move. He knew that it was hopeless, and that Clara and Captain de Beauchesne and the Reverend Mother had all been right.

Early on Friday, they said goodbye to the mission house sisters and took the train back to the convent, sitting side by side in an empty compartment with Ben's misery hanging over them like a rain cloud waiting to explode, and Lotti wondered hopelessly, Oh, what are we going to do?

Sister Marianne had telegrammed ahead, and Clara and Sister Monique came to meet them at the St

Matthieu station in the convent pony cart. Ben shrank away when Clara tried to hug him. She looked at Lotti, who just shook her head.

"I am very afraid," Lotti whispered, "that he is going to break."

At the convent, Ben made straight for the *Sparrowhawk*, where he crept into Nathan's workshop and knelt on the floor by Elsie's crate.

"We didn't find him, Elsie. I'm sorry. We didn't find him."

Gently, Elsie shook away her puppies and climbed out of the crate into his lap. Ben put his arms round her and at last, very quietly, began to cry.

Clara and Lotti sat on the roof with Federico, understanding his need for privacy but wanting to stay close.

"Albert Skinner is in Paris," Clara murmured. "Captain de Beauchesne sent a telegram."

"Skinner!" Lotti's heart skipped a beat, then she frowned, confused. "What's he doing in Paris?"

"I don't really understand either," admitted Clara. "I think Henri—I mean Captain de Beauchesne—arranged it with Madame Royère. In his telegram he says he's trying to deflect him but Lotti, I do think we should go back to England, and the sooner the better really—in the morning. We'll leave the puppies here and take the *Sparrowhawk* to a boatyard to fix that awful rattling, and then we'll get the train home and I will explain to your uncle ..."

"Oh, don't talk about my uncle!" Lotti covered her ears with her hands. "It makes me feel sick."

"Darling, I know you don't want to go, and I understand, but I promise, when we get back to England, I will do everything I can to help you ..."

"You want to *adopt* Ben," said Lotti, accusingly. "Not just *help* him. You said, when you found us in Calais."

"I ... Lotti, have you been angry with me all this time?"

"Yes!" said Lotti. "Mostly I've been thinking about Ben, and about ... other things. But yes, it did *hurt*, Clara."

"But how *can* I adopt you, darling, when you have a family already? I promise you this though, I will look after Federico, and I'll visit you at school as often as I'm allowed. I don't want you to feel alone again, ever."

Lotti kissed her, because she could see Clara was upset, but then she pulled away and said, "It's not enough though, not for me. I want so much more from life than that."

"Lotti ..."

"Let's just sit quietly for now, Clara. Let's not talk about tomorrow. Let's just think about Ben."

It very much seemed, in that moment, as if all was lost.

But once again, they had underestimated the dogs.

Chapter Thirty-Two

The convent hens were happy.

At night, they slept safely in a snug coop with sand on the floor and plenty of shelves for roosting. During the day they roamed freely and laid their eggs wherever they chose. A little bantam called Poulette liked the herb garden. Pauline, her mother, had once laid an egg on the chapel altar. Palinka, an intrepid young russet, flew as high as she could to lay hers in apple trees.

The gardener, Moses, had grown used to finding eggs as he worked, and he liked to look out for them. As he looked, he noticed other things, like caterpillars and butterflies, the discarded nuts of squirrels, tiny red flowers growing in moss, and he forgot all about gardening and eggs but lost himself in these treasures instead. Often on these occasions he smiled, and a dimple appeared in his left cheek.

Moses had been dimly aware of the sound of the cart returning, but he was far away raking a path at the top of the orchard, and had discovered an adder basking in a dip of the wall. He laid down his rake to watch it. The adder was brown and green, looped in elegant coils, beautiful. Moses slowed his breath to match the rise and fall of the adder. Somewhere in the distance, he heard a dog bark, but he ignored it.

His mind wandered.

Around him in the grass, hens scratched at the ground.

Federico was bored. He had hated Buisseau. Shut away with nuns, dragged along sidewalks on the lead. Back at the *Sparrowhawk* he longed to run and explore the woods with Lotti as they used to at Barton, but she was sitting all quiet and subdued with Clara, and had ordered him to sit too.

He obeyed, but it was no life for a dog. And then into the open door in the wall to the orchard there stepped the hen Palinka . . .

. . . who just *stood* there, foolhardy creature, her head cocked coyly to one side, practically *inviting* Federico to chase her . . .

It was too much for any Chihuahua, let alone one who had suffered.

Federico did not hesitate. The *Sparrowhawk*'s roof was high, but this jump was nothing compared to the one at Emlyn Lock. The little dog tucked his legs beneath him and launched himself from the roof of the *Sparrowhawk* onto the jetty, where he bounced, gathered himself and with frenzied barking gave chase.

Palinka, with loud squawks, fled back into the orchard and up the nearest tree. Federico circled the trunk, yapping excitedly. Lotti ran after him, shouting for him to come back. She had almost caught up with him ... her hand was about to close around his collar, when another hen appeared, and then another ... a whole flock of hens at the far end of the orchard! Federico rolled, twisted and streaked away, a toffee-colored blur, bat ears streaming.

Sister Monique emerged at the door of the kitchen, followed by a young nun called Sister Véronique, and then the Reverend Mother. Moses, the gardener, seeing Federico charge toward him, shouted out, a garbled sound, indistinguishable as words, but loud.

On the *Sparrowhawk*, Elsie pricked up her ears.

Federico, oblivious to danger, galloped on. *This* was the life! *This* is what he was born for! *This* ...

Ow!

Moses's blow caught Federico off guard. It wasn't a hard blow—it was aimed to deflect, rather than hurt—and it only clipped his shoulder, but it was enough to send him rolling into the long grass. Dazed, Federico staggered to his feet. Moses brandished his rake.

Federico prepared for war.

Behind him, he heard human voices, Lotti running, now followed by Clara and Sister Véronique. Circling him, there was the gardener with the fierce stick. Behind *him*, there were six fat hens . . .

And now, there was something else . . .

More barking, the thud of familiar paws . . .

Past him, a streak of black, heading straight for Moses . . .

Up went the rake, up and back, aiming at Elsie. Federico prepared to leap to her defense, but it was too late . . .

Elsie had already leaped.

The black and white dog hit Moses full in the chest. He staggered and fell, seeing stars. Barking, strangers, shouting . . . Someone crying. A voice he had heard before, somewhere . . .

Where?

Hot breath on his face. A rough tongue licking his cheek. A whine in his ear . . .

He reached up and sank his hand into thick fur.

In his wandering mind, something shifted.

He opened his eyes. Two wide golden eyes gazed back.

He knew those eyes. He'd known them since she was a puppy.

"Hello, Elsie," he said.

And then a boy was running toward him, and the boy was screaming and sobbing and laughing all at once, and hurling himself on top of him and Elsie so that boy and man and dog were all lying in a tangled heap together in the grass, and Sam said, "Hello, Ben."

Chapter Thirty-Three

Ben began to cry again, not quiet tears now but great, hulking sobs which went on and on as Sam rocked him in his arms, also crying, and in a voice unused for months hoarsely whispered his name, over and over, while Elsie pressed close into them, nuzzling first one brother and then the other.

At last, with a shuddering sigh, Ben pulled away, and looked at his brother, still not able to believe what he was seeing.

"You're here." He reached up and touched Sam's scar. "Does it hurt?"

Sam smiled, a tentative grimace, rediscovering forgotten muscles. "Not anymore."

"I waited and waited," said Ben. "What happened?"

"I'm . . . not sure," croaked Sam.

He looked toward the house, where Lotti with Federico, Clara, the Reverend Mother and a number of sisters had gathered by the back door, witnessing their reunion from afar.

"Come," he said, getting to his feet.

"Must we?" asked Ben regretfully.

"Yes," said Sam. "Not for long. But these women have been good to me, and I think . . . I think the Reverend Mother might help."

When she saw the brothers begin to walk toward the house, Mother Julienne sent all the other sisters away. As Sam and Ben drew close, she held out her hands in a gesture of welcome.

"So, Moses," she said. "Or should I call you Samuel? You have returned."

"I have." Sam's voice quavered. "And I owe you and my brother an explanation. Especially my brother."

The Reverend Mother nodded and then, in her crisp way, offered her parlor as a calm, private place to talk.

Ben pulled on his brother's sleeve.

"Can Lotti and Clara come too?"

"It's not necessary," said Clara, seeing how tired Sam looked. "You'll be wanting privacy."

"But I want to hear," Lotti hissed at her. "Clara! After all we've done to find him!"

"Anything Ben wants is fine with me," said Sam.

In the parlor, under the Reverend Mother's steely eye, the dogs settled angelically on the hearthrug. Lotti sat beside them and pulled Federico into her lap. Mother Julienne, Clara and Sam sat on chairs. Ben sat on the floor close to his brother, as if fearful that at any moment he might disappear again.

In a halting, unfamiliar voice, Sam began to piece together what he could remember of his story.

"Nathan ... he shouldn't have come, but it was so good to see him ... He looked after me, we went for walks, little ones, a bit longer every day, him fussing ... me leaning on him, him leaning on his stick ... it was funny! And then on the day it happened, on the day the planes came ..."

Sam paused. The door opened and Sister Monique appeared bearing a tea tray.

"Just in time," said the Reverend Mother crisply.

After tea had been poured and cups distributed, Sam resumed.

"On the day the planes came, we walked as far as the river, and I ... oh, it sounds so trivial now ... The weather was warm, and I took off my boots because I wanted to paddle and Nathan said ... oh God, I wish I hadn't done it ... Nathan said, you'll be cold, I'll go and fetch a blanket ..."

They all steeled themselves, guessing what was coming next.

"Nathan went to fetch a blanket and . . . well, that's when it happened . . . when the planes came. The last thing I remember was hearing the planes and seeing Nathan . . . seeing Nathan . . ."

Sam began to cry. Lotti stole a sideways look at Ben, saw that he was crying too and felt a lump rise in her throat. Clara was also wiping away tears.

"Go on," said the Reverend Mother.

"Then I don't remember . . . not clearly . . . it's just like pictures, like photographs . . . trees on fire . . . and a nurse with blood on her face . . . and a great hole in the ground . . . and I just . . . I put my boots back on and then I just . . . walked away, following the river . . . I walked for days, and I slept in barns, and sometimes I stole food . . . clothes . . . at some point I must have thrown away my dog tag . . . I didn't talk to anyone, I just walked and walked, and then when I did need to talk to someone I found I couldn't . . . There was a farmer . . . he kept asking me my name, and I couldn't remember . . . It's so strange . . ."

"I believe in English it is part of a syndrome called shell shock," said the Reverend Mother. "It is strange, but also common. What happened next?"

"In the spring I came here, and you were all so kind, and the woods and the river so lovely . . . I think, now, that it reminded me of home, the *Sparrowhawk*, the canals . . . So I stayed."

Ben could see from the Reverend Mother's reaction that she thought Sam's condition quite normal, but he was struggling to understand, and couldn't help feeling a little hurt. "But you must have recognized the *Sparrowhawk?*" he asked. "Didn't you?"

"Yes . . . no . . . I don't know . . ." Sam looked apologetic. "A little, maybe . . . I watched her . . ."

"I saw you," said Clara. "You frightened me."

"I'm sorry," Sam apologized again. Then, looking puzzled, he asked, "How did the *Sparrowhawk* get here?"

"We drove her from England," said Lotti.

"But that's . . ."

"I know." Ben grinned. "Nathan would be livid."

"He would." A slow smile spread across Sam's face, a proper one this time, and Ben breathed a sigh of relief.

At last, Sam looked like himself!

"She took a bashing, the *Sparrowhawk*," Ben said. "She's making this rattling sound. We'll have to check her properly before we take her home."

"I'll come down and look with you now," said Sam. "I can't wait to see the old girl again."

"And Sam . . . Elsie's had puppies!"

At this, the Reverend Mother smiled and stood up.

"In such a moment, I think puppies may be just the thing," she said. "If after all the excitement you are hungry, lunch will be served in half an hour in the refectory. We eat simply here, but there is plenty for everyone, and you are welcome to join us."

She paused at the door. "Ben, Charlotte . . . I have not forgotten what I told you when you first came, that your search was impossible. It appears I was wrong. Well done."

With another smile, the Reverend Mother left. Sam slung his arm round Ben's shoulders.

"Come on then, little brother, let's go and look at these dogs. And the *Sparrowhawk*! Tell me, is the kingfisher still there above my berth? That I *do* remember!"

The brothers followed the Reverend Mother out of the room. Lotti let out a deep breath.

My berth, Sam had said. Well, of course it was. *His* berth. Not hers.

"Let's go and help Sister Monique with lunch," said Clara. "Give Ben and Sam some space."

"Not right now," said Lotti. "There's something I have to do."

Chapter Thirty-Four

Lotti followed Ben and Sam down toward the river. The brothers were deep in conversation. From Ben's hand gestures, Lotti knew that he was talking about the Channel crossing.

He didn't look back to see if Lotti was following. She was hurt, but a part of her was glad.

It made her decision easier.

At the *Sparrowhawk*, she sat quietly on the foredeck with Federico while inside Sam and Ben fussed over the puppies. She listened as Sam walked about the cabins, his conversation peppered with "I'd forgotten" and "I remember."

Ben laughed a lot, and Lotti was glad of that too.

After about fifteen minutes, Ben came out to find her.

"We're going up for lunch, are you coming?"

"In a minute. I'd just like to sit here for a while."

He looked at her and frowned. "Are you all right?"

"I am completely and absolutely fine!" Lotti said. "I'm just being quiet for a bit because it's been such an exciting day. Go! I'll join you in a minute."

She watched him walk away through Nathan's workshop with quick, elastic steps she had never seen before.

"Ben!" she called, just before he reached the door into the cabin.

He stopped and turned. "What is it?"

"I'm glad we were friends."

Ben laughed, then left.

The strangeness of Lotti's parting remark didn't strike Ben until he stood before the convent's refectory table, listening to the Reverend Mother say grace.

I'm glad we were friends, Lotti had said.

Not *are* friends.

Were.

What was that supposed to mean? And why wasn't she here?

They sat down to eat, and Lotti didn't come.

"Where is she?" asked Clara.

"She said she wanted to be quiet for a bit."

Clara looked worried. "That's unlike Lotti."

Yes, thought Ben. It is.

Suddenly, he had a very bad feeling. He pushed back his plate.

"I'll just go and make sure she's all right."

He knew something was wrong the moment he stepped on board the *Sparrowhawk*. Lotti wasn't on the foredeck and the cabin hatch, which he'd left open when he went to lunch, was closed. He pushed it open, and Elsie began to whine, then shot past him onto the rear deck and began to bark, facing the path which led past the door of the orchard wall into the woods.

Ben went down into the cabin.

At first glance, the *Sparrowhawk* seemed exactly as he had left it earlier. His unpacked bag lay where he had slung it on his berth. There was a half-drunk glass of water on the fold-down table, beside a copy of *Great Expectations* Clara had been reading. But something was missing . . .

"Oh no."

Lotti's berth was neat as a pin, the pillow plumped, the blanket smoothed and folded back.

But her mother's soft blue butterfly shawl, which had covered the bed from the day she moved in, was gone. Ben opened the drawer at the foot of the berth where

Lotti kept her clothes, but he already knew it would be empty.

Elsie was still on the rear deck, barking toward the trees. Ben knew exactly what she was telling him.

Running faster than he had ever run, Ben headed into the woods. As he ran he seethed with rage, first with Lotti for leaving without an explanation, then with himself for not understanding earlier that she was saying goodbye.

I'm glad we were friends.

But why?

After a few minutes, he spotted her through the trees, walking resolutely along the path with her rucksack on her back and Federico beside her. He yelled her name, and she stopped. Ben's lungs were burning but he carried on running until he reached her.

"What are you doing?" Lotti looked upset. "I didn't want you to follow me."

"What am *I* doing?" he panted furiously. "What about you?"

She raised her chin. "I'm going to find my grandmother."

Ben was bewildered. "I didn't even know you *had* a grandmother!"

"Well, I do," said Lotti calmly. "She lives in a town called Armande, and I'm walking to the station to catch the train to go there."

"But ..." Ben sat down on a tree stump, too baffled to stand. "Why didn't you say?"

"Well, I didn't know myself for sure until we got back from Buisseau," Lotti admitted. "It's an idea that's been growing. You see, she stopped writing to me shortly after my parents died ..."

"Why?"

"I don't know," said Lotti. "But earlier today, Clara said something that made me think; I can't go home until I've spoken to her. Not until I'm sure."

"But why didn't you say anything?" Ben felt an almost overwhelming desire to cry. "You didn't even say goodbye!"

Lotti looked a little ashamed. "Frank didn't say goodbye."

"At least Frank left a note!"

Lotti bit her lip. "Well, you have Sam now ..."

"So you thought I didn't need you anymore!" Ben's expression was thunderous. "You thought I was like your grandmother who stopped writing to you, or like your horrible uncle, that I could just ... *throw you away!*"

"No!" Lotti looked stricken. "No, I never thought

that! Not really. Just, you all want to go home, and Clara thinks I should go too, and . . ."

But Ben was fully launched.

"Well, I'm not like your uncle!" he shouted, quivering with indignation. "Do you think I'd let you go on your own after everything you've done for me? To a horrible old woman, who stopped writing to you when you needed her? We are going back to the *Sparrowhawk* RIGHT NOW and then me and Sam are going to FIX HER and then we are taking you to your grandmother ON the *SPARROWHAWK* because that is WHERE YOU BELONG and if she isn't nice to you I WILL THUMP HER!"

He glared. Lotti, trembling, began to laugh, then tried to say something and burst into tears instead.

"Does that mean you *won't* go on your own?" Ben demanded.

"No! I mean, yes! I just thought . . . oh, never mind. I think I *am* used to people throwing me away, like you said . . . and I'm used to doing things for myself . . . but oh, Ben, thank you! I'm so scared, you know, that Moune won't want to see me; that she'll turn me away or send me back to Barton. It will be so much easier if you're with me."

Ben, fighting a fresh urge to cry, said, "We'll ask the

sisters if they have a spare mattress or something. We can put it in the workshop."

"How crowded we'll be!" said Lotti. "Eleven of us, and we started with just four!"

"We'll need more food," said Ben. "Maybe the sisters could spare some. And we'll have to look at the map ..."

Smiling and full of plans, Ben and Lotti walked together back toward the *Sparrowhawk*, but as they arrived their faces fell.

Clara and Sam were standing on the jetty, and Clara was holding a telegram.

"It's from Henri," she said when they reached her. "Albert Skinner's on his way to Buisseau."

Lotti swallowed. Ben looked at her. She was scared, and with good reason—there was barely a household in Buisseau that didn't know their story.

"We'll leave straight away," he said.

"What?" said Sam.

"I'll explain later. Sam, get your things. We'll say goodbye, and we'll go."

"But the *Sparrowhawk* ... you said she needed fixing."

"She'll be fine until we get to Lotti's grandmother."

Clara's eyes widened. "Lotti's ... ?"

Oh, why did grown-ups always have so many *questions?*

"WE NEED TO GO," Ben yelled. "BEFORE

ALBERT SKINNER GETS TO BUISSEAU AND SOMEONE TELLS HIM WE ARE HERE!"

Clara and Sam exchanged looks.

The *Sparrowhawk* left the convent within the hour, waved off by the nuns.

Because she loved Sister Monique and now wouldn't drink anything but goat's milk, they left the little puppy Delphine behind, as a token of their thanks.

PART V

Chapter Thirty-Five

Ever since the *Sparrowhawk* left, visits to the convent had not stopped.

The first to come, on the morning after her departure, was a grumpy Englishman, completely bald under his flat cap, and wearing an ancient patched jacket. He came by the river on a small, Belgian-registered motorboat, and he spoke no French. The nuns took him to the Reverend Mother, who spoke to him in private, then Sister Véronique accompanied him back to the river and stayed to wave goodbye.

Next, a few hours later, came Henri de Beauchesne, roaring up on Madame Royère's cousin's motorbike. He did not even enter the convent, but spoke to a gaggle of nuns out in the courtyard. Had the English travelers come? They had? And left one of the puppies? Goat's milk! How extraordinary. And had they found the English boy's brother? A gardener! It was like a miracle. Captain de Beauchesne could hardly believe it. And they had received his telegrams? And had she—they—all of them—returned to England? No? Did the good sisters know, by any chance where she—they—all of them—had gone? He had to find her, he said, finally giving up all pretenses that what he cared about more than anything in the world was Clara. He could not live without her! He roared off again as soon as he had his answers, waved on his way by an admiring crowd.

The good sisters felt no concern about either of these visitors, knowing they meant the travelers well.

But now there was this English policeman.

Henri de Beauchesne, when Albert visited him in Paris, had been very apologetic but completely unhelpful. He remembered the *Sparrowhawk*, of course—such an odd boat, who wouldn't?—but he had not seen her since Calais. After leaving Henri's apartment, Albert had walked for a long time through Paris, thinking. With no knowledge of *where* the *Sparrowhawk* was, he asked himself *why* she was in France. What had possessed Ben and Lotti to undertake such a perilous journey? In

Albert's experience, the two most common reasons for such extreme behavior were fear, and love. You didn't need to be a detective to work out what Albert's fugitives were afraid of: Ben was afraid that his lie would be found out, and Lotti (understandably, thought Albert) was afraid of her uncle. But why France?

Love, love, love . . .

Ben has gone to look for his brother, John Snell had said. Could it be that . . .

Albert Skinner sent a telegram to his colleagues in Great Barton:

WHERE DID SAM LANGTON GO MISSING?

He left for Buisseau two days later, as soon as he received the answer, arriving just a few hours after the *Sparrowhawk* had left the convent.

The next morning, he walked to the bombed hospital site in search of clues, and sat by the river as Ben and Lotti had. As he contemplated the ruined landscape, Albert thought of his son, lying in his nursing home with his gas-damaged lungs, screaming with nightmares every night, and his mind wandered past the scene before him to another river long ago where his son had paddled as a child, and he sighed heavily for all that was lost.

Back in Buisseau, still shaken from his reminiscences, he sat in the café in the southwest corner of the main square, where the waiter who had refused to serve Lotti brought him a cup of coffee. It was Saturday, market day. As Albert drank, he noticed a small crowd gathered around a nun carrying a basket. Curious, he approached to look . . .

"It was the fault of Delphine!" wailed Sister Monique, back in the convent kitchen. "And of Federico, with the ears! She looks too much like her father! And now the policeman is with the Reverend Mother, and she will tell him everything."

"You should not have taken Delphine to market," grumbled Sister Véronique.

"You know how she cries whenever I leave her! She is a tyrant, that one—worse than Napoléon, or my aunt Florence who made everyone take a siesta after lunch every day, even at Christmas. And that policeman, he is clever. I did not think Englishmen were clever like that. The way he interrogated me! *Excuse me, Sister, where did you get that puppy?*—except in English, I had to ask Monsieur Gautier from the café to translate—and I was not able to lie!"

Sister Monique punched a lump of bread dough.

"Is there any chance," she wondered, "that the Reverend Mother might lie?"

Sister Véronique just looked at her.

Albert Skinner left the convent for the railway station at St Matthieu, there to catch a train to Armande.

Nobody waved goodbye to him.

Trains being substantially faster than narrowboats, Albert arrived in Armande within a few hours. He took a room in a hotel by the river, with a window overlooking the quayside, from which he could see any boat arriving or departing from town. A swift inquiry confirmed that the *Sparrowhawk* had not arrived. Satisfied, Albert sent a telegram to Hubert Netherbury, to inform him of what he had discovered.

Hubert Netherbury's fury on learning that Lotti had absconded from school was nothing compared to his rage when he found out that she was heading to Armande.

He replied to Albert Skinner's telegram by return.

ON NO ACCOUNT ALLOW CHARLOTTE TO
SEE HER GRANDMOTHER . . . STOP . . .
GRANDMOTHER GRAVE DANGER . . .

STOP ... LEAVING IMMEDIATELY ...
STOP ... WILL ARRIVE ARMANDE LATE
SUNDAY AFTERNOON ... STOP ... I
REPEAT, CHARLOTTE MUST NOT SEE HER
GRANDMOTHER ...

Less than an hour later, Hubert Netherbury was on a train pulling out of Great Barton station.

And the race was on.

Chapter Thirty-Six

Lotti adored the *Sparrowhawk* but oh, why was she so slow?

A day and a bit to reach Armande, Ben had reckoned from the map. They had hoped to arrive late on Saturday, but now it was past lunchtime on Sunday and they were still not there. Lotti sat with Federico on the foredeck, willing the *Sparrowhawk* on. She knew that Ben and Sam were pushing her as hard as they dared, but the little narrowboat had given almost all she had to give. The rattling in her hull had grown worse, and she crawled along at a walking pace. She might have fared better on the still, calm waters of a canal, but they were traveling on rivers, buffeted by swirls and eddies and unpredictable currents. The river they were on since this morning was wide and strong, and now they had to contend with increased traffic as well, and the wake of much larger boats. Lotti knew from the glances Ben and Sam exchanged that they were worried, and they were so kind to be taking her to Armande ... But somewhere out there was Albert Skinner, the policeman who never gave up, and somewhere behind Skinner there must be her uncle too, and beneath the fear of both of these, all the time, was the fear of Moune's reaction when she saw her.

Lotti felt sick just thinking of it.

The door to the foredeck opened and Clara came out, carrying a mug of tea.

"Drink," she said, passing Lotti the mug. "And stop worrying."

Clara was being kind too, making meals, making tea, she hadn't once mentioned going back to England. Everyone was being kind ...

But oh, *why* couldn't the *Sparrowhawk* go faster?

It is a widely accepted fact that the best way to approach Armande is from the water and from the east, where the river swoops round a wide bend and the town, with its ancient bridges and Gothic architecture, its tall cliffs topped with timber-framed villas, presents itself in all its glory. True, you can get a similar effect from the road, which at this point runs alongside the river, but the view is better from the water. To this end, a private company in this first summer after the war had set up a paddle steamer to run up and down the river, charging tourists for the view. And it was the wake of this steamer that finally did in the *Sparrowhawk*.

She passed the *Sparrowhawk* at a good clip a mile short of Armande, just before the bend in the river. The waves she threw up were nothing like the waves on the Channel, but they were strong enough to rock the *Sparrowhawk*, and now to the rattling inside her hull a ghastly creak was added, as something deep inside gave way.

Once she began to take on water, the *Sparrowhawk*'s end was fast. There was just time for Sam to bring her to the bank. Clara held fast to the mooring lines while Elsie and Federico ran up and down the shoreline and the others salvaged all they could—the puppies in their crate, the splintered robin and the kingfisher, Nathan's books . . . rucksacks, clothes, the three tin mugs . . . Clara was struggling to keep the *Sparrowhawk* alongside the riverbank. Sam jumped ashore to help her, and Ben tore about the cabins alone, panicking, seizing what he could . . . a box of paints, a frying pan, a pillow, a blanket . . . passing them up through the cabin hatch to Lotti on deck as all the time his mind shrieked at him that this couldn't be true, this couldn't be happening . . .

"Ben! Lotti!" Sam shouted. "You have to get off! You have to get off now!"

For the last time, Ben and Lotti leaped from the deck onto the bank. Then, with an awful groan, the dear *Sparrowhawk*, where for nine years Ben had felt safe and loved, which had carried him and Lotti so bravely on their quest to find Sam—the *Sparrowhawk* disappeared underwater.

For almost a full minute no one but the barking dogs made a sound.

Damp, bedraggled, their shoes and clothes dripping muddy river water, Lotti and Ben stood clutching each other.

"It's my fault," said Lotti at last in a strangled voice. "If I hadn't wanted to come here, if I hadn't been in such a hurry . . ."

"No, no, no," whispered Ben. "It's my fault. I'm the one who said she could make it . . ."

"It's nobody's fault," murmured Sam. "The old girl broke doing what she's always done, rescuing people. It's what she was best at."

"Poor *Sparrowhawk*." Clara swallowed a sob. "Poor, brave *Sparrowhawk*."

The sun, which had disappeared behind a cloud, came out again, glinting on the water, and everyone's behavior shifted. Only Federico remained where he was, absolutely still, watching the spot where the *Sparrowhawk* had gone down, as if expecting it at any moment to break through the water and reappear. Elsie left the shoreline to return to her puppies. Sam and Clara began to gather the rescued items from the shore. Lotti and Ben let go of each other to help. In due course, they would mourn the *Sparrowhawk* fully, and think about what came next. For now, her loss was too much to process. It was only possible to think about what they should do this minute, and in the minutes which followed.

From the road behind them came a rumbling sound, loud and intrusive, but they ignored it.

Lotti said, in a tiny voice, "Maybe my grandmother will let us all stay with her. How far is it now to Armande?"

Ben, his voice equally small, said, "About a mile."

"We can walk it," sighed Clara, but nobody moved.

Behind them, they heard footsteps.

"Oh, what *is* it?" cried Clara.

She turned, and gasped.

On the side of the road above the riverbank stood a motorbike. And walking toward them, untying his leather helmet, came its rider ...

Henri de Beauchesne looked less splendid than he had on the ferry crossing when he'd first met Clara. His journey from the convent had been fraught. The motorbike had broken down twice, he had gotten lost three times and he had slept in a barn. He was tired, unshaven and his clothes were stained with engine oil. As he strode toward the group by the river, removing his goggles and helmet, he felt suddenly very nervous, unsure of his reception, worried that in coming here he had offended Clara, that he should have stayed away. Nevertheless, he spoke with as much confidence as he could muster the words he had come all this way to say.

"Please, Mademoiselle Clara ... may I help?"

The captain, having been quickly apprised of the situation, immediately became efficient.

"I will go to Armande and send a car to fetch you and your belongings," he declared. "Where should it go? To your grandmother's house, Lotti? No, that is a bit much perhaps, so many people and dogs at one time, after all these years. The quayside then, which is famous in Armande. And Lotti—no, do not argue, I know how independent you are, but it seems from what you have told me that time is of great importance here—I will take you to your grandmother alone."

"On the motorbike?" asked Ben, with a stab of envy.

"Of course on the motorbike," said Henri, very seriously. "Perhaps later if I may be useful to you, I can take you somewhere also?"

He looked at Clara and added, with a return of his earlier nervousness, "Will that be acceptable, Mademoiselle Clara?"

Clara nodded, and smiled, and kept on smiling as, a few minutes later, Henri left on the motorbike with Lotti, bound for her grandmother's house.

On the quayside at Armande, Albert Skinner waited.

Chapter Thirty-Seven

Lotti had never ridden a motorbike before, but she was too full of emotion to pay attention to how it felt. The war had barely touched Armande. Over the wide stone bridge they went where she had sometimes fished with Papa, past a waterside park where Mama had liked to walk. Skirting the quayside where Albert Skinner waited with his eyes on the river, they entered the town, zoomed past the covered market where Papa had once bought Lotti a secret éclair, round the main square with its Gothic cathedral where they came for Easter Mass, and with each familiar landmark Lotti held on a little tighter to Henri. On the corner of the square, Henri stopped a cab and ordered the driver to fetch the others, and then the motorbike began to climb up, up through steep cobbled streets toward the clifftops, and Lotti couldn't breathe but clung to Henri as though to a life raft.

Moune's house was the last at the end of a pleasant tree-lined street, separated from the road by a stone courtyard full of roses, just as Lotti remembered, with a shady garden at the back. Henri stopped by the side of the road and Lotti climbed down. She was shaking, but it had nothing to do with the motorbike ride.

That everything here should still exist as if nothing had changed!

"What if she won't see me?" she whispered to Henri.

"Why shouldn't she see you?" he replied.

"But what if she's not *happy* to see me? What if she's angry? What if she sends me back?"

"Then you'll be no worse than you are now, will you?" he reasoned. "Come on, Lotti. You've made it this far; you're not going to give up now. It can't be worse than that storm on the Channel."

Gently but firmly, he took her by the shoulders and turned her toward the house.

"You're right," said Lotti. "I'll do it quickly, before I lose my nerve."

"Want me to come with you?"

"No, it's all right. I'll do it on my own."

Lotti took a deep breath, then, ignoring her jelly legs,

walked fast across the courtyard to the house. The front door had been painted green, which was new, but the knocker in the shape of a lion's head, which had delighted her as a child, was still there. Lotti grasped it, breathed again, then rapped three times.

A stern, middle-aged woman in a housekeeper's dress and apron answered the door.

"Yes?"

Lotti's heart sank. The housekeeper was looking at her exactly the same way the waiter at the café in Buisseau had, like she was some sort of street urchin. Too late, she wondered if she should have changed her clothes.

Well, she couldn't do anything about that now. Lotti raised her chin and, in her most defiant voice, announced that she had come to see Madame St. Rémy.

"Madame St. Rémy is resting," replied the housekeeper, coldly. "She cannot be disturbed."

Lotti faltered. "Would you mind ... please could you ... could you tell her that her granddaughter is here?"

Madame's granddaughter! Well, that settled it. The housekeeper had not worked long for Madame St. Rémy, but Madame kept a photograph of her granddaughter on her desk, and the child looked nothing like this. Madame's granddaughter was a pretty little thing with long shiny curls, pleasingly dressed in the sort of frock in which rich English people liked to show off their children.

She was not an *urchin*.

The housekeeper blamed the war, which had caused people to become desperate and crime rates to soar. Thieves would try anything to trick you out of your money. Just outside the gate, she spotted a rumpled-looking man with an eye patch, who had clearly slept in a ditch and was obviously an accomplice.

Nonetheless, if there was the slightest chance . . .

"Do you have proof?" asked the housekeeper.

"Proof?" stammered Lotti.

"A passport maybe, something like that?"

Lotti felt all the color drain from her face.

"I . . . I don't," she gabbled. "I mean, I had one but . . . the thing is, I was on a boat, and it sank, and . . ."

"A likely story," said the housekeeper.

"Oh, please!" begged Lotti. "There's a policeman after me, and . . ."

The housekeeper closed the door in her face.

Dazed, Lotti returned to Henri and told him what had happened.

"What shall I do now?"

"What do you want to do?"

"Wring her neck," said Lotti fiercely. "Kick down

the door. Or scream and scream until Moune wakes up. Horrible old bat! The way she looked at me!"

"I'm not sure that would help." Henri looked at Lotti appraisingly. "I must say, I don't think I'd believe your story either if you turned up on my doorstep. Come on, the others must have arrived by now. Let's go and get your things and tidy you up and come back when your grandmother's awake. We'll bring Mademoiselle Clara with us too. She can vouch for you."

"But *Constable Skinner* . . ." wailed Lotti, her fierceness deserting her. "*My uncle* . . ."

"Uncles and policemen be damned," said Henri. "I'll protect you."

And so back on to the motorbike climbed Lotti, and back down the winding road she went with Henri de Beauchesne, past the square and the market to the quayside, and there, just coming out of the taxi, were Ben and Sam and Clara and the dogs with all the things rescued from the *Sparrowhawk*.

Henri pulled up beside them.

"Well?" asked Clara.

"Slight hiccup," said Henri. "We need to tidy Lotti up."

Muttering under her breath, Lotti began to rummage through her rucksack. Was there anything, *anything*, which didn't look as if it had been pulled from a jumble pile? And why did it matter? Must she really dress up, pretend, play respectable for a housekeeper? This wasn't what she had run away for! Dimly, she was aware of Federico barking, of Elsie joining him, of Ben shouting... She heard a boat engine rumble then go quiet, footsteps approaching and then the dogs barking louder, a grumpy voice saying, "Well, Federico, well, Elsie, it's good to see you again," and Ben sort of gasping and laughing, and at last she looked up and squealed because it was Frank, returned from Belgium.

"It was something you said, Charlie," Frank explained, after Lotti had hugged him and Ben had shaken his hand and Sam and Henri and Clara had been introduced. "After I saw my brother's grave, I got thinking. See, Jack always wanted a dog. And I thought about payment. I never did feel quite right about our deal. So I came looking for you and"—he rummaged in the inside pocket of his jacket—"I thought I'd give this back and ask if I couldn't have one of them puppies instead."

And into Lotti's hand he dropped the ring that had been in Théophile's family since before the Revolution...

Albert Skinner missed the arrivals of Lotti and Henri and Frank for the most prosaic of reasons. He'd been watching out for the *Sparrowhawk* all day without moving, and he was absolutely bursting for the bathroom. He returned to his window just in time to see Lotti fling her arms round Frank.

Albert should have run, gone charging out of the hotel to snatch Lotti, waving an arrest warrant. But he couldn't move, couldn't take his eyes off the young man with the scarred face and tattered clothes standing with his hand on Ben's shoulder, looking considerably older than twenty but alive, more than alive, actually smiling ...

Was this Sam Langton?

And could his own boy, his son, one day smile like that again?

A motorbike revved, breaking the spell. Albert's eyes flicked toward it and he swore softly. The driver in his helmet was almost unrecognizable, but there was no mistaking the eye patch. So Captain de Beauchesne was part of this too, was he? Albert chastised himself, realizing how the captain had fooled him in Paris. But now Lotti was climbing onto the back of the motorbike, and Albert shook himself.

He had come to France to do a job. He had disliked Hubert Netherbury since their first encounter, when Lotti's uncle had ordered him to fetch Federico, and his dislike had grown with each of their subsequent exchanges. But his job wasn't to like people, it was to uphold the law, which in this case meant ensuring the safety of an absconded minor.

Albert ran out of the hotel, past Sam, Ben and Clara, who looked aghast, and into the road, where he hailed a passing cab and managed despite terrible French to instruct the driver to follow the motorbike.

He was in luck. Henri, with Lotti riding behind him, drove carefully. Albert's driver, promised an extra tip for speed, did not. The cab screeched up outside the clifftop house just as Lotti climbed off the back of the motorbike. Thrusting a handful of notes at his driver, Albert jumped out of the cab.

Chapter Thirty-Eight

For a brief moment, before Lotti noticed him, Albert
had a clear view of Lotti's face, and what he read on it
took his breath away.

Fear, certainly, or at least apprehension, but also ...
hope.

Fierce, burning, furious hope.

Then she saw him, and hope vanished, replaced by
fear.

Henri turned, glowered and stepped forward to
protect Lotti, but Albert made no move toward her.

Instead, Albert stared.

Albert stared, and Albert stared, and Albert stared.

Puzzled, Lotti stepped away from the motorbike, and
began to walk toward the house. She reached the porch,
then stopped and turned to see if he was following.

Albert continued to stare.

Lotti squared her shoulders. Once again, she reached for the lion's head, and knocked. Once again, the housekeeper opened the door. For a moment, it looked like she would close it again. But then Lotti held out the ring . . .

The housekeeper scowled, but she took the ring and went back into the house, closing the door firmly behind her. Lotti waited, her heart in her mouth. At the gate of the villa, Henri and Albert stood side by side now watching.

The door opened and a tiny, silver-haired woman in her late sixties came out. There was a cry—Albert knew that he would never forget that cry.

The cry was surprise and disbelief and longing and joy and grief all rolled into one, but most of all it was love.

The silver-haired woman opened her arms, and Lotti fell into them.

Albert Skinner, with a nod to Henri de Beauchesne, walked away. Back down the hill he went, all the way to his hotel, where he checked out before boarding the next train to Paris, and then the boat train to England and his son.

"Dangerous," Hubert Netherbury had written about Lotti's grandmother in his last telegram, but now that he had seen Camille St. Rémy, Albert didn't believe it for a minute.

Lotti's grandmother cherished Lotti in a way Hubert Netherbury never could.

And if there was one thing the war had taught Albert, it was that children were to be cherished.

"He lied to both of us."

Camille St. Rémy and Lotti sat in the back garden on a little terrace under a vine-covered gazebo, holding hands on a wicker sofa Lotti remembered well from scores of summer afternoon naps as a little child. A tray laden with tea and cakes lay before them, brought by the slightly shamefaced housekeeper and untouched because neither grandmother not granddaughter could bear to let go of each other.

"I wrote and wrote," Camille said. "All of that first year, every week like I promised, even though you didn't answer. I thought perhaps you were too little, that I shouldn't expect a reply, but eventually I wrote to your uncle to ask if anything was wrong, if you were all right. He replied asking me to stop writing to you. He said my letters reminded you too much of your parents, that you had told him you wanted to forget them, to forget me ... He said they upset you too much, that you cried uncontrollably when you read them ..."

"But I never did receive them!" Lotti cried. "I wrote to you every week as well. When your letters stopped, I couldn't understand it. I thought you must not love me anymore. *He* said you didn't love me anymore!"

"As if I could stop loving you!" said Moune. "Oh, I should have known it wasn't true, I should have trusted you, but he was so forceful, so adamant . . ."

"He must have stopped forwarding your letters to me when I went to school," said Lotti, thinking. "And at school, the housemistresses read all our letters. He must have ordered them to stop my letters to you. But why?"

Camille sighed. "I think I know."

And then she told Lotti something Lotti had never known—that in their will, Théophile and Isobel had made it clear that should the arrangement with the Netherburys prove unsatisfactory, Camille St. Rémy should be given full guardianship of her granddaughter, and take over responsibility for Barton Lacey.

"But why couldn't I just live with you in the first place?" asked Lotti. "I would have much preferred that."

"Your parents thought it would be better for you to have a younger guardian," Camille explained. "And also that you would prefer to stay at home in England. Of course, they never imagined that any of this would be necessary . . . As to your uncle, it was better for him if you and I were separated. He sent you away to have Barton all to himself, then made sure you and I never spoke so I never learned of his cruelty to you. My poor darling, were you really away from home for so long?"

"Four and a half years." Lotti rubbed her cheek, then in a small voice asked, "Moune, you won't send me back, will you? I can come and live with you?"

Her grandmother hugged her very close.

"I will never send you away," she whispered. "I promise with all my heart. But now, Lotti, *chérie*, I need you to explain. How did you come to be here, alone, with this extraordinary haircut and these strange dirty clothes and your papa's ring? What *has* been going on?"

Lotti grinned.

"If I tell, you won't believe me," she said. "But first, Moune, there are quite a lot of people I need to introduce you to ..."

Hubert Netherbury arrived in Armande as expected, late in the afternoon. Furious to discover that Albert had already left town, he ordered his hotel concierge to fetch him a cab and went straight up to the house on the cliff, still bent on preventing a reunion between Lotti and her grandmother.

Hearing voices from the back of the house, he walked a little farther along the road to peer through the hedge.

In the garden, a party was taking place. On the sofa under the gazebo, he saw Camille St. Rémy, older than when he last saw her at his sister's funeral but just as formidable, sitting with . . . Hubert did a double take . . . Lotti's tutor from Great Barton.

Both women were looking very serious. Hubert wondered uncomfortably if they were talking about him.

He looked beyond them to the lawn, where a rowdy game of *boules* was taking place, led by a disheveled but splendid-looking man with an eye patch, and at the heart of the game, dressed disgracefully and with an outrageous new haircut, he saw his niece.

There might be time yet, thought Hubert uncertainly, to get her back. With enough confidence, he could march into the garden and order her away. He was still Lotti's legal guardian, after all . . .

From the other side of the hedge, he heard a nasty growl. Looking down, he recognized the horrible little dog he had ordered to be shot at Barton Lacey.

"Shh!" Hubert hissed. "Go! Go away!"

But Federico did not shush, and he did not go away. Instead he began to bark. At the sound, Lotti looked up. Seeing her uncle, she paled. Ben, noticing, came to stand beside her.

"We can thump him if you like," he whispered. "There's enough of us."

But Lotti shook her head. Then, raising her chin, she looked her uncle directly in the eyes.

"That won't be necessary," she said with a smile. "I've already won."

EPILOGUE

Ben and Lotti

The party went on late into the evening. Cake and tea gave way to champagne and sandwiches, and now the housekeeper, whose name was Janine, was rifling through the kitchen cupboards with Henri and Clara, looking for something for supper, Frank was asleep on the lawn, and Sam and Moune were playing with the puppies. Lotti and Ben slipped through the hedge with Federico, onto the cliff, where they picked up a path leading through trees to a ledge looking out over the river.

"Papa's secret place from when he was a little boy," Lotti said. "We used to come here to watch the sunset. It's so strange to be back without him. Don't look down, you'll get vertigo."

"After all we've done, I think I can cope with a bit

of vertigo," Ben scoffed, but he pressed his back against the cliff face because the drop down to the river was very high and steep.

They sat for a while in companionable silence, watching the boats on the river below, while Federico explored the clifftop.

"What a long way we've come," said Lotti at last. "The canal, the Thames, the Channel . . ."

". . . the convent, the hospital, the river . . ."

"Did you see, Ben, earlier, the captain and Clara holding hands?"

"I did," said Ben. "And I'm glad."

"And how Janine went all soft when she saw the puppies, and how Frank drank too much champagne . . ."

"Is that why he's asleep?" grinned Ben.

". . . and how Federico and Moune absolutely adore each other? Darling Federico, with a proper home at last."

They were silent again, but now the silence was different, because their whole lives had changed and they hadn't talked about it yet.

"Poor *Sparrowhawk*," said Ben.

"Will you get her back?" asked Lotti. "Is that even possible?"

"Sam is going to talk to the river authorities tomorrow," said Ben. "But it's unlikely, and even if we do, she won't survive another Channel crossing. We have to go back to England though. Sam's not actually discharged from his regiment yet, and he says there's paperwork, and then he has to get a job, and I have to go to school and we have to find somewhere to live, but I don't want to go."

"I have to go to school too," sighed Lotti. "Though it probably won't be so bad, if I can come home every day. Ben!"

"It's not goodbye," said Ben firmly. "I won't let it be. I'll run away again if I have to!"

"No, Ben, listen! I've had such a good idea. If Moune is right and she can become my guardian and Uncle Hubert moves out of Barton Lacey, *you* can live there with Sam, and Zachy!"

"Me and Sam, at Barton Lacey?" Ben began to laugh. "That's mad. Your grandmother wouldn't let us!"

"Why shouldn't she?" demanded Lotti. "She loves you. And anyway it's *my* house."

"Your uncle might not agree to any of this."

"We'll make it happen," said Lotti. "You and me, we've done it before. We'll never really say goodbye, even if we live in different countries. And meanwhile, Ben, listen. There's a whole summer before school starts, and Moune says you can stay here as long as you want. And, look . . ."

"Where?"

"Can you lean over, just a bit? Do you see that building, down below?" She pointed to a low wooden riverside structure. "That's a boathouse. And in the boathouse there's my father's old boat, the one I told you about the first time we met. It's just a rowing boat, nothing fancy like the *Sparrowhawk*, but Moune says with a bit of work it will be absolutely fine to take out. She even thinks we could have an engine fitted. Frank could help us with that, while he waits for his puppy to be old enough to take back to England. Moune says, if we want it, it's ours. What do you think, Ben? You know, if we keep going west, we could reach the sea. There are marshes there like on the Thames, and huge beaches, and at the right time of year, there are seals . . ."

Ben listened, his head touching Lotti's as she talked on, sketching out her plans.

Living at Barton Lacey! Summer holidays in France! Seals, and going west all the way to the sea!

It was mad. It was preposterous!

It was . . . *irresistible*.

Far below, the evening sun lit up the water.